MUSTANG SUMMER

MUSTANG SUMMER

•

JANE McBRIDE CHOATE

AVALON BOOKS
THOMAS BOUREGY AND COMPANY, INC.
401 LAFAYETTE STREET
NEW YORK, NEW YORK 10003

Library of Congress Catalog Card Number: 94-94533
ISBN 0-8034-9073-9

PRINTED IN THE UNITED STATES OF AMERICA
ON ACID-FREE PAPER
BY HADDON CRAFTSMEN, SCRANTON, PENNSYLVANIA

To Cathy Forsythe

Thanks for being there.
Together we did.

Chapter One

The stallion stood guard as his mares grazed nearby.

Brad stared in reluctant admiration at the beautiful animal. Years ago, he'd named the horse Conquistador. The Conqueror.

It fit.

Brad let his gaze linger on the mustang, taking in his proud bearing, flared nostrils, and shiny coat so dark that it appeared inky black against the dun-colored landscape. Conquistador was as much a part of this land as were the lizards and scrub brush.

Brad knew this bold conqueror almost as well as he knew himself. They were old enemies. And friends. The inconsistency didn't bother him. He respected Conquistador, just as he would respect any man—or animal—who fought for what was his.

Conquistador had been king of Salt Flats for years. Once he'd led a herd of mustangs as wild and free as himself. Now, he had to content himself with mares stolen from ranchers' herds and some straggly crossbreeds.

Instinctively, the mustang knew where the best grass

grew and where to look for water. He knew how to find shelter from the harsh winter winds that blew undeterred across the prairie. He was a master at escaping the scores of men who'd tried to put a lasso around his neck and a brand on his hide. Many a time a rancher had followed Conquistador into what appeared a box canyon only to realize the mustang had found an escape route.

Brad had never been among those who tried to capture Conquistador. He'd listened to the stories of men who'd matched wits with the horse and had secretly cheered Conquistador's escapes. Brad valued his own freedom too much to deny it to anything so untamed as the mustang.

Until now.

Conquistador had crossed the line. He'd taken Brad's mares, mares he'd planned to breed to improve his stock.

"You've gone too far this time, my friend," Brad said, the softness in his voice at odds with the hard look in his eyes. "Why didn't you stay where you belonged?"

He looked at the rope that lay in his hands, useless now, broken by the fury of the stallion when Brad had had the temerity to loop it around the horse's neck. It had held taut until Conquistador had pitted his strength against it.

Brad knew he wouldn't get another chance. Not

today. The stallion was too cunning to be taken in again. Even now, the mustang raised his head and pricked his ears, as if sensing danger.

The pounding of hooves pummeling the drought-hardened ground had Brad turning in his saddle. He watched as two of his men rode up. They wore the same rueful expressions that shadowed his own face.

"Sorry, Boss," one of the men said, taking off his hat and wiping his forehead with a sweat-stained kerchief. "He's a wily devil."

"Yeah." Brad tilted back his own hat.

"It's supposed to get hotter tomorrow," the man said, uncapping his canteen. He took a long drink, the water dribbling over his chin and down his neck.

Brad opened his own canteen and let the water trickle down his throat. "So what else is new?" Besides the fact that Conquistador had stolen three more mares. Besides the fact that some bureaucrat was due to arrive today to start tagging the mustangs. Besides the fact that there were always too few hours in the day to do everything that needed to be done to keep a ranch the size of his going.

He watched as the men exchanged wary looks. "Sorry," he said. Whatever his problems, he didn't have the right to take it out on his men. "We'll try again tomorrow."

"Sure thing, Boss."

Brad knew they were waiting for him, but he motioned them on. He needed some time alone right now. "I'll see you back at the ranch."

He watched as they rode off until they were no more than a puff of dust in the distance. Heat shimmered in waves, causing him to pull his hat down to shade his eyes.

Shakespeare neighed, an impatient reminder that he didn't like the inactivity.

"Okay, boy," Brad murmured. "We're going home."

Conquistador had beaten them. For today. *There'd be another time*, Brad promised the proud stallion.

The mustang trumpeted his victory with a loud whinny, a signal for his mares to follow. They lifted their heads from where they'd been grazing. A shrill whistle ensured their obedience.

Brad swept off his hat, a silent salute to the victor. He didn't delude himself that it would be easy to capture the mustang. Nor did he want to. Conquistador belonged to the wind. But this time, he wasn't leaving Brad any choice.

"Dr. Freeman, you're sure about this?" Dr. Samuels, area supervisor of the Society for Western Conservation, asked.

Jamie Freeman nodded, resisting the urge to fan herself with the sheaf of papers he'd pressed upon her. Montana's climate, she'd read, was cool and pleasant during the summer. Apparently, the weather hadn't read the same tourist brochures she had.

"You understand what we're trying to do?" The little man with the pitted skin and nervous manner didn't wait for her answer but continued. "If you're successful, we'll be able to preserve the last of the mustangs by establishing a registry for those that carry an unbroken line of Spanish blood." He cleared his throat, drawing her attention to his Adam's apple, which jutted forth prominently. "I don't have to emphasize the importance of the task."

"No, you don't." Tagging and protecting the few mustangs remaining in the state had been her dream for as long as she could remember. This was her chance, and she didn't intend to give it up.

"You're very young for such a job. When I was told the brass was sending someone, I expected someone older, more experienced."

Jamie kept a tight rein on her temper. The officious little man was treating her as if she were straight out of the schoolroom. She knew, better than most, the importance of protecting the few mustangs left.

He pushed his glasses down on his nose. "I hadn't expected a woman."

"My sex doesn't have anything to do with how I do my job," she said evenly. "I'm a professional."

"Yes, yes." His tone made it clear he believed just

the opposite. He scrubbed a hand through his thinning hair. "I'm afraid the salary for the job isn't much."

That was an understatement. Apparently, the Society for Western Conservation believed their employees could live on devotion for their work alone.

"I know. I'll manage." Jamie fixed him with a steady gaze. "Is there anything more?"

"No, no. You're free to go. Of course, you'll report your findings to me."

"I was under the impression I was to report them to the main office."

"Well, yes, but I'd like to have a look at them and then send them on."

"You'll have to get permission from the president for that. Until then, I'll send whatever I find to the Society itself. I'm sure you understand the need to follow rules."

"Of course. Of course." He wiped his hands on his pants.

Jamie controlled the urge to run out of the stuffy little office, away from its stuffy little resident. The man was so nervous he'd nearly wrung his hands.

She held on to her patience. If she had to work with the high-strung Dr. Samuels with his outdated ideas about women, it was a small price to pay for the chance to live out her dream.

For twenty-six years, she'd prepared for this. She'd grown up on stories of the old West. Ever since she could remember, her grandfather had regaled her with tales of roundups, cattle drives, and rodeos. He'd outlived the days when cowboys and their horses were the backbone of the sprawling cattle ranches; now they had been replaced by pickup trucks and helicopters.

But he'd instilled in Jamie the excitement, romance, and energy of the era. The seeds he'd planted had taken root, and she'd known from an early age that she'd return to this land someday and make it her home.

She remembered the sadness in his voice when he'd told her about the bounties put on mustangs to rid the land of them. The ranchers had banded together and set out to exterminate the mustangs. His eyes had filled with tears as he recalled how a single packer had slaughtered over a third of a million "fuzztails," the ranchers' names for mustangs.

The carcasses had been sold to manufacturing plants that turned out products like fine-grained cordovan leather, glue, and fertilizer. Now the once-proud horses that had roamed the west in herds numbering in the thousands were reduced to a pitiful few.

If she could complete this project, it would go a long way toward righting the wrongs that had been committed over a half century ago. Only a few hundred mustangs existed in the state, and those that did were regarded as nuisances by the ranchers.

Jamie felt her excitement growing as she bid a hasty good-bye to Dr. Samuels. Billings, where Samuels's office was located, was only fifty miles from the town of Dream's End. She hadn't been back to the small town since her grandfather had died over ten years ago, but she felt as if she were coming home.

On her way once more, she scanned the road for signs to Dream's End. The road stretched in front of her, a ribbon of gray that unrolled over the barren landscape. Surely, it couldn't be far now. Just as she thought her arms would drop off from sheer exhaustion, she saw the sign: DREAM'S END—5 MILES, NEXT EXIT.

A sense of exultation swept over her—she was nearly there. She hadn't been here in over ten years, but she knew she'd come home. A narrow road, hardly more than a path, led to her grandfather's house.

The house was smaller than she remembered. She gave it only a cursory glance before changing into jeans and a shirt, ignoring a brief twinge of guilt. She should check out the house, unpack her belongings, and do any of the dozen things that needed to be done when moving into a new place. But the land drew her; the harsh plains and ragged peaks were far more appealing than the mundane chore of unpacking.

She'd give herself an hour. Only an hour, she promised, to do some scouting around. After all, she couldn't go far on foot, and she had no intention of seeing the country for the first time from the inside of her car.

Shading her eyes from the sun, she peered into the

distance and saw a cloud of dust. Could she possibly be lucky enough to catch a glimpse of the mustangs on her very first day? Telling herself not to expect too much, she headed in that direction, her sneakered feet quickly covering the ground.

She wasn't sure how far she'd gone, but the cloud had disappeared. Sighing, she decided to head back to the house. A large root caught the toe of her shoe, and she felt herself falling. She landed hard, the breath knocked from her. When she looked up, a large shadow loomed over her—a big man astride an equally big horse. She watched as he dismounted and walked toward her.

She started to push herself up when a large hand closed around hers and pulled.

"Thanks." She paused a moment to take a gulp of air before holding out her hand. "I'm Jamie Freeman."

"Brad Kincaid." His hand, large, tanned, and callused, swallowed hers.

She gave herself a moment to study him. He fit here, not just in the way he was dressed—the leather vest worn over a denim shirt and the jeans faded to near-white—it was in the way he held himself, the way he was at one with his surroundings. His skin was brown like the land, his eyes bluer than the Montana sky.

"I'm here from the Society for Western Conservation." She smiled, but the tall cowboy didn't return it. She felt more than heard his quick intake of breath.

Puzzled at his abrupt coolness, she said, "I'm here to identify and track the mustangs."

"I know."

So that was it. Well, better to meet the opposition up front. That way, she knew what she was facing. "I take it you don't approve of what I'm trying to do."

"You take it right. People around here don't have much use for thieves, especially the four-legged variety."

"Thieves?"

"That's right. A band of wild mustangs has been making off with mares from the ranchers. My herd was hit a couple of days ago."

Her brow wrinkled. "You're running your stock on an open range?"

"Look around you. We're in the middle of a drought. I *have* to use every bit of range I have just to keep my stock alive."

She followed his gaze and saw what he meant. The sun-scorched ground, with its almost nonexistent vegetation, was mute evidence of the drought.

"How long's it been going on?"

He swiped at his face with his bandanna. "A couple of months."

"Your mares—did you find them?"

He rocked back on his heels, thumbs hooked in his pockets. "Yeah. I found them."

"So what's the problem?"

"Finding and catching are two different things. Or are you such a city slicker that you don't know the difference?"

Her chin came up. "You've got a chip on your shoulder, Mr. Kincaid."

"Make it Brad. And it's no chip. What I've got is a good, old-fashioned mad."

"I understand that losing your mares could make you angry."

"Angry doesn't begin to cover it. Conquistador and his marauders took three of my best mares. One was in foal."

"Conquistador?"

"The leader. A black stallion." She watched as his eyes softened. "I named him that a few years back. He has all the arrogance of one of the Spanish conquerors, just like his ancestors."

"You like him?"

His eyes hardened once more. "I did."

"Did as in past tense?"

"You got it."

"I'm sorry about your losses. But that doesn't change what I have to do."

"Have to or want to?"

She lifted her chin another notch. "It's my job. I intend on doing it."

For the first time, Brad smiled. "You don't back down easy, do you?"

She responded to his smile in spite of herself. "No. Did you expect me to?"

He shrugged. "I didn't know what to expect. I heard they were sending some kind of expert with a fancy Ph.D. to identify the mustangs."

She waited as he gave her a thorough scrutiny.

"Whatever I expected, though, it sure wasn't you."

"Let me guess. You expected a little man in glasses with his head bent over a clipboard and his nose stuck in a book."

The smile deepened. "How'd you know?"

"I get that a lot."

"Must be the doctor in front of your name."

"Must be."

His smile died. "I respect what you're trying to do, but you don't understand what you're up against." He pointed to the horizon, a strip of purple that banded the prairie. "See that?"

She let her gaze follow where he pointed, trying to understand what he was talking about.

"The land," he said impatiently. "The land. It's what this is all about. The land is a living thing. It's what makes us what we are."

"We?"

"The people who make their living from the land. And that means just about everyone around here. The land's a part of us. When something threatens it, we fight back. We have to."

The impatience had left his voice. It was quiet now. Quiet and controlled. But something else lay just beneath. She tried to pinpoint what it was. Desperation. Fear.

He wouldn't admit to it, she realized. A man like Brad Kincaid wouldn't like acknowledging anything akin to weakness. Even without knowing him very well, she sensed that. He was proud and stubborn.

She was beginning to understand his attitude toward the mustangs. It didn't change what she had to do, but she softened her tone and reached out a hand. "Listen, Mr. Kincaid—"

"It's Brad," he reminded her.

"Okay. Brad. I understand how you feel, but—"

"You have no idea how I feel. How could you? You're barely here a day and you think you know how I feel?" The impatience was back. In spades.

Too late, she recognized how pompous her words must have sounded. She was a newcomer here. She knew enough to realize it would take a long time for her to be accepted. If ever. Her grandfather had lived here for ten years, and he had still been considered an outsider by the locals.

"I'm sorry. I didn't mean to offend you." She took a deep breath and decided she'd better get it over with. "But I'm here to do a job. I'm sorry if it bothers you, but I believe in what I'm doing."

"I like that," he said, surprising her.

"Like what?"

"That you don't back down from doing what you think is right."

"Then you won't try to stop me?"

"I didn't say that." He leveled a long look at her. "You have a job to do. So do I."

Confused, she tilted her head back in order to see him better.

Blue eyes caught her gaze and held it until she broke the contact. "Can I give you a ride home?"

"No, thanks."

He touched his hand to his hat and unhurriedly started back to his horse. He mounted the big gelding with enviable ease and rode away, leaving Jamie to stare after him.

The man was an enigma. Cool and aloof one moment, warm and friendly the next, angry and disapproving the next. She had a feeling she could like him under other circumstances. She shook her head and sighed in regret. Fate had put them on opposite sides of the fence.

The late afternoon heat beat down on her, and for a moment, she regretted the pride that prompted her to refuse his offer of a ride home. Her once-white sneakers were a dusty brown by the time she reached the house, and she mentally added buying a pair of boots to her growing list of things to do.

She inspected the house and sighed. Well, she'd

known the house was run-down after years of being empty, but she hadn't expected it to be *this* dilapidated. Now, she wished she'd thought ahead and hired someone to clean the place up before she arrived.

Cobwebs clung to the corners, dust coated the few pieces of furniture, and a stale, musty smell clung to the air. Neglect and decay were evident everywhere.

She unpacked a bare minimum of things and set to work. Four hours later, she stood back and surveyed her efforts. The house was still shabby and run-down, but at least it was relatively clean now.

A glance at her watch confirmed what her stomach had told her hours ago. It was late. She spared a few minutes to heat a pan of soup before tumbling into bed. But though her body clamored for sleep, her mind churned over the events of the day.

Her emotions had run the gamut from exasperation with Dr. Samuels to excitement over her new job to annoyance with Brad Kincaid. Strangely, it was the latter that her thoughts focused on. And, she admitted, it wasn't only annoyance she'd felt.

She'd been intrigued by him. His obvious love for the land was something she could understand and respect. Hadn't her grandfather felt the same way? He'd believed the land was a trust, passed down from one generation to the next. No one could own it, he'd told her more than once, only care for it and preserve that heritage for the next generation. He'd passed on his love for the land and the mustangs to her.

That brought her full circle to the thing that had brought her here. The mustangs. She had a job to do. And she didn't intend on letting anything—or anyone—interfere with that.

For a moment, she knew a pang of regret. Brad Kincaid was someone she would have liked to get to know better. But she feared their loyalties would always divide them. Her thoughts churned around and around until she could stand it no longer. She slipped on a robe and let herself outside.

A velvety darkness closed around her; a breeze feathered over her face. She'd forgotten how different things were here than in the city. The night was thick and black, emphasizing the brilliance of the stars. In the city, the stars were frequently lost in the glitter of lights. Here, nothing interfered with nature's splendor.

Then too, there were the sounds. The chirping of crickets, the scuttling of a small animal, and the buzzing of insects created a harmony that rivaled that of renowned symphonies. She remembered the noises that routinely bombarded her ears in the city. Horns blasting, sirens screaming, and engines roaring were a poor substitute for the music that serenaded her now.

Reluctantly, she headed back to the house. She had a big day planned for tomorrow, and she had a feeling she was going to need every bit of energy she had—and then some.

Morning light came early here, she decided as she rubbed her eyes. A glance at her clock told her it was only 5:30 A.M., but the rosy light of dawn was already pushing away the last of the night's darkness.

Her muscles protested as she climbed out of bed. She'd expected to fall asleep immediately last night, but the events of the day had replayed through her mind with the precision of a video recording. She'd known she'd face opposition for the job she came here to do, but she hadn't counted on encountering it so soon.

She shook off the doubts that had pestered her during the night and grinned as she remembered her grandfather's words: "Don't go borrowing trouble, gal. Do what has to be done and the trouble will take care of itself."

"You were right, Grandpa," she whispered.

The pipes in the tiny bath sputtered ominously as she turned on the hot water for her shower. She didn't dare linger, so she shampooed her hair and rinsed it, praying the water would hold out. Back in her bedroom, the floorboards were cold against her feet, and she dressed quickly. That was another thing she'd forgotten—how cold mornings in the country were. An apple left over from yesterday's lunch would have to do for breakfast.

Some checking in town netted her the name of a stable. With the directions written down, she drove there and made arrangements to rent a docile-looking mare named Mustard Seed for as long as she needed the animal. From the stable owner, she got a lead on some out-of-work ranch hands who might be willing to help her capture and tag the mustangs.

With a quiet sense of accomplishment, she headed back to town and parked outside the local hardware store, a modern version of the old-fashioned general store. Intent on buying a pair of boots and a hat, she failed to hear the voice that called her name.

"Hold on, Jamie."

When she turned and saw Brad striding toward her, she waited.

His long legs soon covered the distance between them. He waited while she finished her shopping. Following her outside, he asked, "What are your plans now?"

She wrinkled her nose. "Before I can start looking for the mustangs, I've got to set up my computer so I can write down my findings."

"How about having lunch with me?"

With growing hunger pangs and an aversion to starting the paperwork without which the Society for Western Conservation seemed unable to function, Jamie was tempted to agree.

He held out a placating hand. "I came on pretty strong yesterday. I'd like to make it up to you."

"I . . . okay," she said.

He took her arm and led her to a western-styled restaurant, the tables covered with red-checkered oilcloth. After they were seated, he summoned a waiter. "Frank, we won't need menus today. Two orders of ribs, fries, and salads."

"Yes, sir, Mr. Kincaid."

"They do the best ribs around," Brad said when the waiter had disappeared.

When Frank returned shortly with a platter of barbecued ribs, Jamie gasped. They each appeared to be as long as her arm.

"Just use your fingers," Brad advised, observing her struggles with the knife and fork. "It's the only way."

Gingerly she picked up one rib and bit cautiously into it. "It's delicious."

They ate in companionable silence, licking sauce from their fingers and wiping their faces with the plentiful supply of napkins.

Brad subtly directed the conversation. "How did you get hooked up with the Society for . . . what is it again?"

She laughed. "Society for Western Conservation." Her smile faded as she recalled the grueling schedule of attending classes at night and working during the days. "I started college studying biology and conservation. When I got out, I wanted a job in which I could use both. An opening at an animal protection agency came up. I worked there while I completed my doctorate and ended up here."

"It sounds tough."

"Yeah, it was. But it was worth it."

Companionably, they cleaned up the platter, fries, and salad. She realized she'd told him almost everything about herself and learned nothing about him.

"What've you decided about the project?" His abrupt question rattled her.

"I'm going ahead with it. Did you think you could talk me out of it?"

"No." He took her hand, lacing her fingers through his. "You probably won't believe this, but I'm thinking about you as well as the ranchers. You want to make a life here for yourself?"

She nodded.

"Word spreads fast around here. If you do what you're intending, you're going to destroy any chance you ever had of making friends here." He glanced around. "People here have long memories. They're reserving judgment about you so far because of your grandfather, but . . ."

The quiet sincerity in his voice convinced her he was telling the truth. But it didn't change what she had to do. She looked at their linked hands, his darkly tanned, hers only faintly so. Each was strong yet different . . . as different as she and Brad.

"I know my job's not going to win me any popularity contests."

"But you intend to go ahead."

She nodded. "I have to."

At some point, their hands had fallen apart. A symbol, she wondered, of the differences that divided them, and always would?

Brad looked at her for a long moment. "I suppose you do."

Was that regret she saw in his eyes? "I have to do what I think is right." Suddenly, it was important that he understand how much this meant to her. If he could accept that, then maybe . . .

Her hopes died at his next words.

"So do I." He signaled for the check, put a couple of bills down on the table, and stood.

Battle lines had been drawn. The truce was over.

Chapter Two

Her new boots pinched her feet as she walked outside the following day. An early-morning chill penetrated her thin cotton blouse. She knew that the temperature would soar soon enough, though, as the sun climbed higher into the sky.

She headed to the barn where she'd settled Mustard Seed yesterday. She'd been drawn to the mare immediately, liking the look of quiet intelligence in the horse's eyes. Now, as the little mare waited patiently while Jamie fiddled with the saddle and reins, she knew she'd made the right choice.

"I don't know what we're going to find today, girl. And I'm new around here, so I'm depending on you to not get us lost. Okay?"

She took Mustard Seed's whinny as agreement.

Jamie held out a map, frowned over it, and then stuffed it back into her shirt pocket. The questions she'd posed in town had netted her nothing but polite—and some not so polite—rebuffs. She'd studied maps of the area and zeroed in on the canyon just west of her property as a likely spot for the herd to graze. She settled her hat more firmly on her head, nudged the mare with her heels, and started off.

An hour later, she was watching for any sign of the mustangs. Never one of her virtues, her patience was being stretched to the limit as she waited.

For a moment, she allowed her attention to wander as she reflected back on those words. *Her property*. She'd never thought of herself as a property owner, but she realized she liked the idea. Especially since that land had once belonged to her grandfather. When he'd died, the land had been sold for back taxes. Since then it had traded hands several times. It had taken ten years and every bit of her savings to scrape together enough for a down payment.

It had been worth it.

"You've got dirt running through your veins," he'd told her more than once. "The kind of dirt that makes you itch to touch it, run your fingers through it, get your hands dirty with it."

She hadn't understood what he'd meant at the time. Her grandfather had often talked in riddles.

But she'd taken his words to heart. She'd played cowboys and Indians instead of house, asked for chaps and a hat for birthdays and Christmas rather than dolls, and counted the months until summer when she would see her grandfather again.

He'd made sure she respected the land as well as loved it. She remembered a picnic when he'd taken her to one of the canyons. As they prepared to leave, she carelessly tossed the trash to the ground. Quietly her grandfather cleaned up the area, leaving it as pristine as when they came. He'd never said a word to her about the incident. He hadn't needed to.

A pounding of hooves alerted her to the approach of the mustangs. Her breath caught in her throat now as she saw them for the first time.

"Beautiful."

The word escaped in a small gasp as she watched the leader of the herd, a black stallion whose glossy coat gleamed brightly against the stark landscape. The small head, delicately formed and arrogantly proud, proclaimed his Spanish blood.

She remembered her grandfather telling her that the name mustang comes from the Spanish word *mesteño*, meaning unclaimed or belonging to the range. Watching Conquistador, she understood that. He belonged to the land as surely as did the prairie grass and mountains.

A half-dozen other horses bore a striking resemblance to him. Probably his offspring, she decided. Most of the rest were a straggly-looking bunch of crossbreeds. With blood from various breeds, the mustangs had become an odd assortment of mongrel horses.

She noted a half-dozen or so well-fed, sleek-looking mares in the herd. Brad's missing mares, she guessed. And probably a few belonging to other ranchers.

She wasn't prepared to try to do anything with the horses today. For now it was enough that she'd spotted them. She spent another fifteen minutes watching them and admiring the stallion.

Could he be Conquistador?

He fit the description that Brad had given. Now she understood the note of respect she'd heard in his voice. How could anyone not admire such a magnificent animal? How could anyone want to deny him his freedom?

The sun beat down with merciless intensity. She pushed her hat back and let the slight breeze cool her forehead. Untucking the kerchief from around her neck, she wiped the perspiration from her face and thought ruefully of the full canteen she'd left sitting on the kitchen table.

Only a tenderfoot went off without a canteen.

The nickname brought a smile to her lips. Her grandfather had called her that the first summer she'd spent with him. It had been a source of pride that he hadn't had cause to apply it to her again. From the time she was ten until his death six years later, she'd spent every summer here.

Her smile faded as she realized how far away from the land she'd grown in the intervening years. She'd rationalized her long absence by reminding herself she'd been busy with getting her education and starting a job, but she knew it was more than that. She hadn't been able to face the memories.

This land was so tied to her grandfather that she couldn't think of one without remembering the other. It had taken her several years to get over his death. She shook away the sadness and reminded herself of her promise to remember the good times.

Enchanted, she watched as the colts in the herd bucked and cavorted in the sun like frisky puppies. They butted each other with their heads, pranced off, and returned to start the game all over again. After a while, they nursed at their mothers' sides and nickered to each other. The soft sounds reminded Jamie of a baby nuzzling at his mother's breast.

One mare, probably the lead mare, bossed her way through the herd and picked out a spot with the greenest grass. She tossed her head and neighed, warning the other horses away. When a few remained, she nipped at them until they fled in cowed defeat. Her colt nestled down beside her.

It was like a small community, Jamie thought, complete with leaders and followers, rules and regulations.

Her attention focused once more on Conquistador. He was the most beautiful animal she'd ever seen. He was also cautious, she noted as she saw his ears flick forward. What had he heard? She listened intently but couldn't hear anything except for the rustling of the wind.

Conquistador neighed, a piercing call to his herd. The mares lifted their heads, nudged their foals to their feet, and prepared to follow. Just then another stallion, a rare blue-gray colored called *grullo*, appeared. He pawed the ground in unmistakable challenge.

She watched in growing horror as the two stallions pranced around each other. The big gray had youth on his side. But Conquistador was a master at putting upstarts in their place. He wouldn't be easily beaten.

His silver tail held high and neck proudly arched, Grullo, as Jamie had named him, whinnied loudly, an unmistakable taunt. She shifted her attention back to Conquistador.

His head lifted a notch. He had heard the challenge. And accepted it.

The sparring had stopped. Conquistador waited. It was not for him to initiate the battle. He was, after all, the king.

Ears laid back and teeth bared, Grullo charged. He lashed out with his hooves. Head lowered almost to the ground, he weaved it back and forth, nipping at the other's forelegs.

Conquistador reared on his hind legs and kicked out his feet. Jamie held her breath. Blows from either side could cripple the opponent.

Over and over, Conquistador attacked the upstart. Finally, head bowed, Grullo stumbled away, but not before Conquistador gave a call of triumph.

Jamie hadn't realized she was holding her breath until now. She expelled it in a low whistle.

"Magnificent, aren't they?" Brad asked.

Startled, she turned in the saddle. She'd been so engrossed in watching the battle that she hadn't even noticed his approach. "I've never seen anything so wild. Or so beautiful."

"One goes with the other."

"You're right."

He tipped his hat back. "You sound surprised."

"Not really. I'd just never thought of it that way."

"Most people don't."

She heard the half-sad, half-admiring note in his voice and stared at him, surprised at the feeling she read in his face. He'd been as moved by the display as she had. Encouraged, she laid her hand on his arm.

"Don't you see that they have to be preserved? They're part of—" she gestured with her hands "—all this."

Gently he shrugged off her hand. "Things change. Times change. People change."

"Not you. I hear it in your voice, see it in your eyes, when you talk about the mustangs. You care about them. Just like I do."

"How could you want to destroy something like Conquistador? He belongs here." She spread her arms to encompass the vast plain. Even now, with the land scorched by the unrelenting sun, the prairie was beautiful.

"I agree."

"Then you won't try to capture him any longer?"

"I didn't say that. Conquistador is costing the ranchers around here more than they can afford to lose."

"It all comes down to the bottom line, doesn't it?"

"You better believe it. Ranching isn't some game we're playing at. It's what we do . . . who we are. We can't turn our backs on it because of some romantic ideal."

She turned and knuckled away a tear that threatened to spill over. She wouldn't give him the satisfaction of seeing her cry. She'd fallen in love with the land and the mustangs. Her grandfather had lived and died here; it was her heritage as much as Brad's. And she intended to preserve that heritage, even if she had to fight Brad and all the other ranchers to do it.

"You're wrong," she said, tightening her hands around the reins. She squinted into the distance, absorbing the land that was at the heart of the conflict. It was glorious; it was also harsh and exacting.

A harsh land that demanded an equally harsh man? She didn't need to look at Brad to know where the sun had etched fine lines around his eyes and mouth. But they were only outward signs. She couldn't have been mistaken about his feelings for the mustangs.

He was as much a part of the land as were the wild

horses. They both belonged here. She'd make him see it, make him understand that he couldn't destroy the mustangs without destroying a part of himself. She turned back to him, hoping he'd listen. But his lips had thinned to a hard line, his eyes shuttered against giving anything more away.

She'd learn to recognize that look even in the short time she'd known him, the one that told her to back off. Something had hurt him at one time, something that had nothing to do with the mustangs. Something or someone? The question intrigued her, and for a moment she forgot they were on opposite sides.

"Is it wrong to want to defend what's mine?" he asked.

His question dragged her back to reality with a jolt. She wouldn't get anywhere now, she realized. Some of the day's brightness dimmed though the sun continued to beat down upon them.

"I've got to go."

He made no move to stop her.

She didn't know whether to be grateful or not. She didn't push the mare on the way home. She wanted to take her time and *feel* the land. The land was like the horses she was trying so hard to save, wild and free and unclaimed. A dry wind whipped across her face, stinging her eyes with sand. She brushed it away and then licked her lips, vowing she wouldn't forget her canteen again.

She'd come here to try to preserve and protect the mustangs, but she was beginning to understand that there was much more involved than she ever realized. If she were to do her job, she needed to help find an answer for the mustangs and the ranchers.

The problem gnawed at her for the rest of the ride home. Once there, she couldn't stop thinking about it.

Or Brad.

He'd become wrapped up in the problem. She told herself it was because he was a rancher, but she knew that wasn't the complete answer.

She rubbed down Mustard Seed, taking her time and giving the mare extra attention. The horse nuzzled her neck.

"You're just a big baby, aren't you?" Jamie crooned to the mare, giving her a final pat.

Inside the house, she pulled out a notebook and jotted down what she'd seen today, including the approximate number of horses. It wasn't much, but it was a start. She refused to consider the possibility that she might not succeed.

Brad remained where he was for long moments after Jamie had galloped off, uncomfortable with the thought that he'd been in the wrong. It wasn't a position he was accustomed to occupying. It left him with a bad taste in his mouth. He owed the lady an apology.

Jamie had a right to do her job. If the circumstances

had been different, he'd probably be offering to help her. But, darn it, the circumstances weren't different.

Conquistador and his band were robbing Brad and the other ranchers blind. Another loss like the one he'd experienced last week and he'd be in serious trouble. Given the uncertain price of beef, the losses due to the drought, and the constant outlay for feed, the margin of profit in ranching was minimal even in good years. Add to that the loss of five of his mares, and he was looking at some hard times.

Ever since he'd graduated from college, he'd worked to build the ranch back to what it had been before his father had let it go downhill. It'd taken every bit of energy and every cent he had . . . plus some he hadn't. He'd paid off the last of the bank notes only last year. For the first time in almost twenty years, the ranch was free and clear.

If only he could make Jamie understand what the loss of his mares meant.

Slowly he shook his head. She did understand. He'd seen the quick flare of sympathy in her eyes when he'd told her of the loss. But, as she'd pointed out, it didn't change what she had to do.

Reluctantly he smiled. He liked the lady. She fought for what she believed. Not many men would have stood up to him the way she had. But she was also totally a woman. She was that rare combination of guts and femininity.

His smile vanished, and his face set in hard lines as he remembered his mother. She'd fought for what she believed in too. Only she believed in just one thing—getting away from the ranch and draining it of all its assets. She'd used her femininity to get what she wanted.

Brad had only been twelve when she'd left for good, but he hadn't forgotten his father's despair. At one time, Frank Kincaid had been a respected man in the community. His ranch had been a showplace in the area. But all that changed with his wife's desertion.

From then on, he drank. He drank to forget, to remember, and to stop the pain. Eventually, he drank himself to death. By that time, what was left of the ranch wasn't worth the paper the deed was written on. And the bank held that.

Brad had been nineteen then. A sophomore at college. He'd wanted to come home and help his grandfather start rebuilding the ranch, but his grandfather had refused.

"Get your book-learning, boy," he'd said. "Then come back and show us how we can make this place something we can be proud of again."

Brad had crammed the three remaining years of college into two and a half, worked two part-time jobs to support himself and have enough to send some home each month, and waited for the day he could come back to the land he loved.

They'd been hard years. He hadn't had time for the parties and dates that most of his friends considered so important. Work, study, and more work. None of that had mattered, though. The only thing that had mattered was returning home.

He pushed away the memories, memories that still had the power to wound even after all these years, and stalked back to his horse.

In his office an hour later, Brad drummed his fingers on his desk, the report awaiting his attention untouched.

Why had he let Jamie get to him as she had? Granted, she got under his skin, but that didn't give him the right to ridicule her feelings. She believed in what she was trying to do, just as he believed in what he *had* to do.

He wanted to get to know her better. She intrigued him. A woman tackling this kind of assignment was still unique, even in today's world. A frown blunted his brow. He was more than a little concerned about her. She had no business facing Conquistador or any of the other mustangs alone. He had the uneasy feeling that the Society for Western Conservation hadn't done her any favors in giving her this job.

He stood. He owed her an apology, and he wasn't going to get any work done until he'd made it. He saddled Shakespeare and headed to Jamie's place. If he were lucky, he'd find her at home. If not, well, he wouldn't mind another ride today on the prairie.

He found her in the barn, cleaning out the stalls. He waited several minutes before announcing his presence.

"Jamie?"

She spun around, clearly startled.

"Sorry. I didn't mean to scare you." He felt a slow flush stain his face. "I wanted to apologize. I acted like a bear with a sore paw earlier. I'm sorry."

She extended her hand. "Apology accepted. If you can wait, I'll be finished here in a couple of minutes." She turned her attention back to the mucking out, her lip caught between her teeth as she concentrated on her task.

He found himself smiling as he watched her. She wasn't afraid of getting her hands dirty. He liked that about her. In fact, there were a lot of things to like about Jamie Freeman.

A wisp of short blond hair fell across her face, and she pushed it back, giving him a clear view of her profile. Her cheek was lightly dusted with freckles that she hadn't attempted to hide with makeup.

He dragged his thoughts away from that and reminded himself that he was here to try to make her understand about the mustangs. In the meantime, he might as well give her a hand. He shrugged off his vest, rolled up his sleeves, and picked up a pitchfork.

She spared him a smile before returning to the job

at hand. By the time they were finished, he was adding another piece to the whole that made up Jamie. She wasn't afraid of hard work.

"Thanks," she said, looking up.

Bits of straw clung to her hair. Without thinking, he reached up to brush them away. Even sweat-stained and dirty, she was beautiful. He forced himself to look away and focused on the rough-hewn beams of the barn. Darkened with age, they were silent reminders of a rugged era, of the men and women who'd struggled to survive during that time.

His thoughts took him back to Jamie. It wasn't difficult to picture her as a frontier woman, working to tame the land alongside her man. She'd be a wife, a helpmate, a partner in every sense of the word. Unbidden, images of his mother intruded on his thoughts.

When the silence stretched taut between them, she asked, "Did you want something? Other than to apologize, that is."

He thrust the memories away and dragged his attention back to the present. "I was out of line this morning. You're entitled to your feelings. I had no right coming down so hard on you."

"Maybe it's yourself you were angry at. Because you care about the mustangs."

He threw her a sharp look. "I care about my ranch, about making a living."

"Why is it so hard for you to admit that you don't want to see Conquistador and his band destroyed?"

"I've never wanted that. But I'm a realist. I have to be." He stabbed his fingers through his hair. "Look, Jamie, I know you like them. All city folk think there's something romantic about the mustangs."

"I'm not a city folk—"

He ignored her protest. "Comes from watching too many westerns on TV and at the movies. What they don't realize is the damage they do to the land. It's not just the ranchers who don't like them. They destroy crops too."

"So the farmers don't like them either, huh?"

"No one who makes his living from the land likes them. Conquistador and his herd trample down the range grass and alfalfa fields, eat the rock salt left for the cattle, and kick the life out of sheep and young stock."

He speared her with a hard look. "Aside from everything else, they're competitors for the food. Do you know how much a herd of wild horses can eat? In a drought, with every blade of grass worth more than its weight in gold, that can be disastrous. Not only to the rancher, but to all those who depend on him."

She frowned. "Then we have to find a way to make the land work for the mustangs and the other animals."

"You make it sound easy."

"You make it sound impossible."

He smiled. "Looks like we've got an old-fashioned standoff."

"Looks like."

"Maybe I can convince you to change your mind over dinner."

"Then again, maybe you can't."

"I'm willing to take a chance. What about you?"

She hesitated, knowing he was talking about more than dinner. She felt the tension between them, a tension that had nothing to do with her job. All right, admit it, she told herself. She was attracted to the man.

It was more than the fact that he had dark brown hair that reminded her of rich earth and a lean, rugged build that called up memories of the cowboy heroes of her childhood. It was something much more basic. His love of the land and his reluctance to see the mustangs destroyed despite the fact that they were costing him his livelihood touched something deep inside of her.

Brad nodded, about to say more when a rider hailed them.

"Hey, Brad."

Jamie looked at the sandy-haired young man and then at Brad. The resemblance was unmistakable.

"My brother, Scott," Brad said.

Scott Kincaid dismounted with practiced ease. He walked over to join them and said, "Introduce me, Brad."

Obligingly, Brad performed the introductions. "Jamie Freeman, my brother, Scott. Scott, Jamie Freeman.''

Scott ran an appreciative eye over Jamie, not bothering to hide his obvious admiration. ''We're glad to have you here, Miss Freeman.''

''Thank you. And, please, make it Jamie.''

''Jamie it is then. Brad told me we had a new neighbor. He didn't elaborate, though.'' He chuckled. ''I can see why—now.''

Blushing, she sought to turn the attention away from herself. ''We were just talking about the mustangs.''

Scott nodded knowingly. ''They're nuisances all right. Stole three of Brad's mares.''

''Not you too,'' she muttered.

''Me too?''

''Your brother was just lecturing me on what they do to the land.''

Scott looked uncomfortable. ''Well, Brad's got a point.''

''Does he?''

Scott shuffled uneasily from one foot to the other. ''I don't want to argue with you, but there are two sides to this.''

Brad grinned. ''Spoken like a true lawyer.''

''You're a lawyer?'' she asked Scott.

''Not yet. I take my bar in another year. If . . . '' He looked at his brother.

''No ifs about it,'' Brad said. ''You're taking the

bar and then putting up your shingle. Scott Kincaid, Esquire."

Scott looked uncomfortable. "We'll see."

Something was going on here, Jamie decided. Something she didn't understand.

Brad settled a big hand on her shoulder. "About tonight . . . seven o'clock all right with you? We eat early here in the country."

"I'll be ready."

He sketched a good-bye wave, mounted Shakespeare, and rode off.

She must have been staring after him, for when she turned back to Scott, he was smiling broadly.

"You like Brad."

She flushed. "We just met a couple of days ago."

"He's a great guy."

The undisguised admiration in Scott's tone had her smiling. "You love him a lot."

"Yeah, I do. He's not an easy man to know."

She'd figured that much out by herself. "Did I say something wrong when I asked you about being a lawyer?"

He scuffed the toe of his boot in the dirt. "It wasn't you. It's Brad and me. I wanted to drop out of law school, stay home, and help out with the ranch. Pay Brad back for all he's shelled out to help me. But he won't hear anything about it."

"He wants you to finish school," she said, her admiration for Brad growing as she listened to Scott.

"So do I. But the ranch is getting too big for one man to run by himself. Especially since he started working with the . . ." Looking embarrassed, he said, "I'd better go. I'm glad we finally met, Jamie."

"I am too."

He swung on his horse. With a final wave, he rode off.

What had Scott been about to say? Something about Brad. She had a feeling it was important. Otherwise, why would Scott have dropped the subject like a hot potato?

She started cleaning the tack she found in the corner of the barn. At six, she stopped and looked at herself in distaste. She'd probably need sandpaper to remove some of the grime. Allowing herself a longer than usual shower, she reveled in the unaccustomed luxury. As she reached up to shampoo her hair, her shoulder muscles objected, and she winced.

She slipped on a gathered skirt and a gauzy blouse. A light application of makeup and a flick of the brush through her curls completed her preparations.

Brad arrived promptly at seven. Admiration registered in his eyes at her appearance, and she felt her cheeks turn warm.

A gleaming pickup was parked on the drive. "I had to bring the truck tonight. I hope you don't mind."

The trip took less than ten minutes. When they approached the house, Jamie drew a sharp breath. The house was a perfect complement to its surroundings. Cedar, silvered with age, blended with the land and sky.

"It's beautiful."

He looked pleased. "This is where I grew up."

"You must love it."

"I do."

By unspoken agreement, they put aside their differences. By the end of the evening, Jamie sensed that the job she'd come to Montana to do could cost her more than she'd ever realized. She and Brad were destined to be on opposite sides in her quest to save the mustangs.

Chapter Three

"Steady, boy, steady," she crooned to the stallion. In the week since she'd been working with the roan, she'd spent every available moment coaxing the wary mustang to accept her.

She was taking it slow and easy as she went about the process of tagging the horses. It was important to get the horses to tolerate at least one person so that the tag she'd implanted could be checked and recorded at a future date. Also, if an animal were ever sick or injured, he'd need human help.

The roan, whom she'd nicknamed Red, maintained a skittish distance whenever she approached. He'd allowed her to touch him only once, and even then, with the help of two other wranglers.

But time was on her side. And determination.

Now she adopted the soft, soothing tones she used whenever she talked to the mustang. "You're so beautiful. But you already know that, don't you?"

The mustang whinnied as if in response. She continued the one-sided conversation, all the while keeping a wary eye on the horse. Mustangs were unpredictable.

A blow from a hoof could easily break a bone—or worse.

She inched her way closer and managed to pat Red's neck. To her astonishment, he didn't back off but stood still while she ran her hand across his back.

"See? It's not so bad. Pretty soon you might even like it."

The horse snorted.

"We'll have to work on that."

He pranced away, his head high.

"Show-off," she said, smiling fondly at him. She was drawn to him, despite his contrariness. To her surprise and pleasure, he now approached her cautiously.

"Good boy." She chanced another pat on his neck. Satisfied with the day's work, she backed off. She could undo all her progress by pushing too hard, too fast. Red was coming along.

In the last few weeks, she'd managed, with the help from some of the local cowboys she'd hired on a part-time basis, to capture a dozen mustangs. She'd achieved an uneasy truce with most of the ranchers as she set about doing her job. She was under no illusion that they liked or approved of what she was doing. Maybe, in time, she could find a way to keep the mustangs from raiding the local stock.

Several of the horses had already been returned to the range, the ones that had allowed her to get close enough to implant the identifying tags in the horses' necks.

Red was of sturdier stock. It would take days, maybe weeks, to get him to the point where he'd trust her enough. Until now, she was content just to build the relationship between them.

Her smile died as she thought about Conquistador. After witnessing the battle between him and Grullo, she'd gotten only a glimpse of him. So far, he'd eluded every attempt to capture him. But she wasn't giving up. Conquistador didn't know it, but he was going to be tagged along with the other mustangs.

A sand lizard scuttled under their feet, causing Red to rear.

She jumped out of the way. "Easy," she soothed. "That's right. No one's going to hurt you."

She heard a sharp *whoosh* of relief. For a second, she thought it was her own before realizing it had come from behind her. She whirled around.

"Do you know what could have happened?" Brad walked toward her, his hands on his hips.

She let out a shaky breath. "Nothing happened."

"*This* time."

She was about to tell him that she could take care of herself when she realized it was concern, not anger, that had darkened his eyes to a stormy gray.

"I'm all right," she said quietly.

He closed the remaining yards between them and

placed his hands on her shoulders, as though to make sure she was really all right. His gaze searched her face. He fitted a finger under her chin and studied her face. What he saw there must have satisfied him, for he gave an almost imperceptible nod.

She couldn't help the small tremor that shuddered through her. He drew her close and wrapped his arms around her.

"He's a wild animal. Forget that and you could be dead."

"I'm not likely to forget, but we're getting to be friends. Aren't we?" she asked Red.

The horse had calmed down now, the stench of his fear tapering off in the fresh air.

"You shouldn't be working with him alone."

He continued to hold her, and she wasn't inclined to put an end to it. At least not yet. There was something solid about him that made her feel safe.

"I have a job to do."

"Get someone to help you."

It was time to end the embrace. Gently, reluctantly, she withdrew from his arms, missing their warmth. "Brad, do you take someone with you when you check on your stock?"

He shook his head.

"How about when you mend fences?"

"Of course not . . . " He frowned. "That's different."

"How's it different? Because you're a man?"

He shook his head impatiently. "Because I was brought up on this land. I've seen what can happen to someone who gets trampled by a horse. It's not pretty. If he'd hit you with his hooves . . . "

"You must really think I'm a fool."

"Not a fool," he said gently. "But when a person's totally involved in what they're doing, they may take chances they wouldn't ordinarily take."

She wanted to throw his words back to him, but she couldn't. He was right. She *had* been caught up in her work, not paying sufficient attention to her surroundings. If she had, she might have seen the lizard and guessed at its effect on Red.

"You're right. I should have been paying more attention."

"I just don't want anything happening to you."

"I didn't know you cared."

His lips quirked into a half-smile. "Let's just say you've grown on me."

He gave her a quick kiss, the kind that shouldn't have left her breathless or staring after him even when he'd mounted his horse and ridden away.

But it did.

The 4th of July was celebrated with a town barbecue with beef supplied from the local ranchers. Jamie had volunteered to serve up potato salad and coleslaw at the buffet table. During a lull in the line of people waiting for food, she sank onto a chair and wiped a hand across her forehead.

"You look like you could use this," a voice said.

She looked up to find Scott holding two glasses of lemonade. "You're a lifesaver," she said, accepting one gratefully.

"I try." He hunkered down beside her. "How'd you get roped into this?"

"I volunteered."

He drew back in mock horror. "It's plain you've never been in the Army. The first thing you learn is never volunteer for anything."

"Were you in the Army?"

"Yeah. Four years ago. Joined up when I was eighteen, got my fill of traveling, and knew I wanted to come back here. Uncle Sam's helping put me through law school now. Even with that, though, I couldn't have done it without Brad's help. I don't know how he does it, but he always manages to come up with the money."

"It means a lot to him for you to finish school," she said, remembering Brad's pride when he talked about Scott.

"Brad's always been the one people turn to when they've got a problem. I guess that's why they voted him to the town council. Youngest member they've ever had."

Jamie regarded him with respect. "You really admire him, don't you? You're always singing his praises."

He smiled wryly. "I get carried away sometimes."

She shook her head. "It's nice to see two brothers who so obviously care about each other." She groped for the right word. "It's refreshing."

"And I think you're nice," Scott said.

An unfamiliar voice interrupted her thoughts. "Scott, heard you were back in town."

"Good to see you, Nate." Scott turned to Jamie to make the introductions. "Jamie Freeman, Nate Henderson."

The other man's expression hardened into an unwelcoming stare. "I hear you're trying to save those four-legged varmints."

"I'm here to tag the mustangs," she said. "The ranchers around here have agreed—"

"Well, I ain't one of 'em." He wagged a finger in her face. "I ain't a bleeding heart. Never was and never will be. Don't have no use for those who are."

Sparks flashed from Jamie's eyes. "I'm trying to establish a registry of the few mustangs that are left."

"Rumor is you're trying to save that black devil. He's cost most of us more than one mare. Those animals are ruining good ranches, good men." He wiped a beefy hand across his forehead. "If I lose any mares because of some fool project, I'll . . ."

"That'll be enough, Nate." Brad appeared suddenly, draping an arm around Jamie's shoulders. "Miss Freeman has a job to do. Just like the rest of us."

"Just as long as she knows the score." Nate Henderson stalked off.

Unconsciously Jamie moved closer to Brad. "I'm sorry," she said, glancing around at the stares they'd attracted.

Scott looked embarrassed. "I was just introducing Jamie to Nate when he started in on her. Gosh, I'm sorry, Jamie."

"It's all right." She drew a shaky breath. "I guess I'm not too popular around here."

Brad frowned. "Don't judge all of us on the basis of one man. Nate's not heartless. He's worried about his stock. We all are. Blood stock means the difference between success and failure for a rancher."

"I figured out that much by myself." She glanced about at the other people, all intent on having a good time. "Does everyone here feel the same way?"

He followed her gaze. "Most do. You have to realize that most of the people here make their living from ranching, in some way or other. It's only natural they want to protect their livelihood."

"I understand. I only wish they understood how I feel."

"They understand. They just can't accept it."

* * *

Later, at home, she reviewed the evening. Strangely, the most unsettling event had not been the verbal attack by Nate Henderson, but instead the gamut of emotions she'd experienced when in Brad's company.

Jamie let her thoughts wander back to Brad. He hadn't had to stand up to Henderson on her behalf, yet he'd stuck his neck out for her. She knew he wouldn't win any popularity polls by defending her.

Maybe, just maybe, he was beginning to feel something for her. A smile tugged at her lips as she considered the possibility even as she reminded herself not to read too much into his defense of her. Brad was the kind of man who would always try to do what he felt was right. Still, the idea persisted.

Returning from a grueling ride the following morning, Brad rubbed down Shakespeare, frowning over the lather the big horse had worked up during their ride. Brad had pushed them both hard in an effort to try to come to terms with his feelings for Jamie.

He liked her, genuinely liked her, something he hadn't felt for a woman, aside from Mrs. Milligan, his housekeeper, in a long time. But her job kept coming between them. Last night, he'd stood up for her when Nate Henderson started in on her, but he couldn't help agreeing with the older man about the danger the mustangs posed to the ranchers.

He skipped lunch, preferring the solitude of the barn.

He'd grab a sandwich later. Wearily he rubbed the back of his neck. Tension coiled the tendons there into knots.

A smile chased the shadows from his face as he remembered that today was Saturday. The kids were coming.

''Keep your arms close to your sides,'' Brad said, holding the small boy upright until he got his balance.

''Like this?''

Brad smiled approvingly. ''Just like that. You'll be riding out with the rest of the hands before you know it.''

The boy, Jeremy Wilkins, raised his gaze to Brad's. ''Do you really think so? Could I be a cowboy with hat and spurs and everything?''

Brad patted the small shoulder and made a mental note to find a child-sized hat. ''I sure do. Look how you've taken to it already. You're a natural. Gemma thinks so too.'' He stroked the mare's neck.

Brad swallowed around the tightness in his throat as he watched Jeremy lean over to rub his cheek against Gemma's glossy coat.

They made a few more circles around the corral. Brad stayed close, ready to step in should Jeremy grow afraid. But the little boy adapted to the rocking-horse motion of Gemma's gait, all the while keeping up a steady stream of excited chatter.

"Can we go faster?"

"Sure thing." Brad gave Gemma a light tap on the rump, and the mare started into a gentle trot.

"It's like flying," Jeremy said, clutching the reins. "I didn't know anything could be like this. Up here, I'm just like anyone else."

Brad looked at the rapt expression on the small freckled face. It was one of pure joy. He knew Jeremy had had more heartache than most adults, let alone eight-year-olds, had to face in a lifetime. Yet he faced each challenge with a dogged determination that Brad couldn't help but envy.

They continued circling the corral for thirty minutes. Judging that Jeremy had had enough for today, Brad brought Gemma to a halt.

"Do we have to stop?" Jeremy asked.

" 'Fraid so, partner. But you'll be back next week. If you feel like it, we'll take Gemma out of the corral."

"Can I really?"

"You betcha."

Brad undid the straps that kept Jeremy's legs in place and then carefully lifted him down and carried him to where one of the ranch hands was waiting with Jeremy's wheelchair.

"I think we've got a first-rate rider in the making," Brad said, giving Jeremy a final hug.

"Sure looks like it," the young ranch hand said. "I'll have to watch out for my job. C'mon, Jeremy. I think Mrs. Milligan's got some milk and cookies waiting for you and the rest of the kids.''

Brad watched as the cowboy pushed the wheelchair over the uneven ground. He'd been hosting these Saturday-afternoon rides for handicapped children for over a year now, but the children's delight in the simple act of riding made each time seem like the first.

It hadn't been easy, convincing the head of the orthopedic unit at the local hospital to let him put the program into practice. At first, Brad had been allowed to bring only one child who was being treated on an outpatient basis to the ranch. Now he routinely brought six to eight children there every Saturday.

He liked each of the kids who'd participated in the program, but there was something special about Jeremy. When Brad had first met Jeremy, the boy was living in a foster home and receiving physical therapy twice a week. Now Jeremy was a regular at the ranch.

Jeremy had lost the use of his legs in a car accident that had also taken the life of his mother. His father, grieving over the loss of his wife, had withdrawn into himself with nothing left over for his son.

Perhaps that was why he'd been drawn to the boy, Brad mused. Though their circumstances were different, they'd each known loss. He hoped when Jeremy's father got his act together, he'd come for his son and take him home again. Until then, Jeremy seemed happy enough at the foster home.

Brad's only regret was that he hadn't started the program years earlier. Children with physical disabilities faced a lifetime of limited opportunities. Brad determined that learning to ride a horse was one opportunity they wouldn't have to miss.

He walked back to where Gemma was waiting patiently. "You were a real lady today," he said, patting her affectionately. Gemma was twelve years old and the gentlest of Brad's horses. She was also an old friend.

Brad reached into his pocket and pulled out an apple. She whinnied her appreciation and chewed it noisily. He started to lead her to the barn to rub her down when a voice halted him.

"That was beautiful," Jamie said. She was seated on the fence, her jean-clad legs hooked under the lower rail. She looked like summer with her face flushed from the sun and her hair a cloud of light haloing her face.

"How long have you been here?" he asked, wondering how much she'd seen.

"Long enough."

"Long enough for what?"

"Long enough to see that you're a fraud."

"A fraud?"

"That's right. A fraud. You give a great performance, I'll grant you that, but inside, you're a marshmallow."

He'd been called a lot of things but never a marshmallow. He wasn't sure he liked it. In fact, he was pretty sure he didn't. "You want to explain that?"

"You know. A marshmallow. All hard and crusty on the outside and soft and gooey on the inside."

Not knowing how to answer that, Brad started toward the barn again.

Jamie followed. "That was pretty wonderful what you did with that little boy."

"I took him for a ride. That's all."

"It's not all," she said softly.

He lifted the saddle and blanket from Gemma and began rubbing her down, his hands moving over her sleek back in rhythmic circles. He kept his eyes averted, but he felt Jamie's gaze on him.

"Why didn't you tell me?" she asked.

"I didn't know you'd be interested." It was a lame answer but all he could come up with.

Jamie placed her hands over his, stilling them. "I think it's more than that. I think you were afraid I'd see something you didn't want me to."

"That's crazy." Shaking off Jamie's hands, he moved to Gemma's other side and repeated the process.

"Is it?"

He nodded curtly, uncomfortable with the warmth in her eyes, the softness of her voice. "Don't make me out to be something I'm not. Once a week, I bring some children out to the ranch and give them a ride on a horse. It's not a big deal.'' He picked up a curry comb and began grooming the horse.

''It takes a special man to do what you're doing. To give up your Saturdays for a bunch of kids.''

Impatient, he turned around and faced her. ''There's nothing noble about it. The kids get a kick out of it, and so do I. That's all.'' He stopped. He had no call to talk to Jamie that way. No call at all. She'd only been interested, and he'd turned his temper on her. ''I'm sorry. It's just that . . . ''

''You don't want people knowing about it.''

''That's part of it, but not all. Plenty of people know what we're trying to do here—doctors, physical therapists, social workers. But I've tried to keep it pretty low-key. If the newspapers got a hold of it, they'd be out here, taking pictures, turning it into some kind of sideshow and making the kids out to be freaks.'' He took a long steadying breath. ''They're normal kids who've had some tough breaks. But on a horse, they're the same as anyone else.''

He smiled, remembering Jeremy saying the same thing to him only a few minutes earlier. ''That's what this is all about. It's showing them that they can—with a few limitations—do anything they put their minds to.''

Jamie touched his arm, her fingers warm even through the denim of his shirt. ''Your secret's safe with me.''

He looked at her clear eyes and knew she was telling the truth. She could no more lie than she could turn her back on the mustangs she was so determined to help.

"Thanks."

"You're welcome. Maybe, someday, you'd let me help you with them."

How many times had he wished for an extra pair of hands to help with the kids? Scott and the ranch hands helped when they could, but they were usually needed elsewhere if he was to keep the ranch a paying concern. "You'd do that?"

"Of course I would."

There was no mistaking the compassion in her eyes. Her heart was as big as the Montana sky with enough room for a bunch of kids she'd never met.

"What brings you out here?"

"I need your help."

"With what?"

Her eyes were now clouded with worry. "Nate Henderson is making trouble with the ranch hands I hired, trying to talk them into quitting. I tried talking to him, but he won't listen. I thought if you talked to him—"

"You know enough about horses to understand what breeding stock means to a ranch," he replied. "If a rancher's to build up his stock, he needs mares. A mare in foal is worth thousands of dollars."

She nodded. "I know. But I also know that Conquistador and the others like him are fighting for survival.''

''So are the ranchers. Conquistador's been around for years, but he's always minded his manners. Up until now.''

''What caused him to start raiding the ranches?''

Brad shrugged. ''Your guess is as good as mine. I'd say, though, that last winter killed off a good deal of his herd. He's probably looking to restock it. That's why he's only taking mares.''

Jamie nodded.

Brad saw the unhappiness in her eyes. It wouldn't hurt to talk with Nate. ''I'll see what I can do. But I'm not making any promises.''

''I'm not asking for any. If I can return the favor . . . ''

''You can.''

She waited.

''I need someone to help me pick out a present for Mrs. Milligan.''

''Your housekeeper?''

He nodded. ''It's her birthday next week. I never know what to give her, so I usually end up giving her a check. But this time I'd like to make it more personal.''

She smiled. ''I'd be happy to. When do you want to go shopping?''

''Monday all right?''

She nodded.

"I'll pick you up in the morning. We could go into the city and make a day of it. If you have time, that is."

"I'd like that."

The smells of horse and hay surrounded them, but suddenly Brad wanted very much to kiss her. He drew her to him. She smelled of sunshine and a faint, elusive scent that reminded him of honeysuckle.

He lowered his head. His lips met hers in a sweet union that caused him to catch his breath. She fit him perfectly, her head coming just up to his shoulder.

The kiss, which he'd intended only as a light peck, stretched into seconds and then into minutes. When he released her, he was trembling. Never before had a woman affected him this way . . . until now. Until Jamie.

At home, Jamie thought about Brad's patience with the little boy. He'd shown a side of himself that she'd never seen before. Not that it surprised her. She'd known for some time that he wasn't as hard and tough as he made himself out to be. He was caring and compassionate, warm and generous.

He'd been uncomfortable with her witnessing the scene. She smiled, remembering how he'd lifted the boy from the horse, settling him into his wheelchair with infinite gentleness. His hands had lingered on the boy's shoulders as Brad had knelt by the wheelchair to whisper something to him.

Brad was a complex man with as many sides as there were colors in the sky at sunset. Drawn by the idea of observing another of the spectacular Montana sunsets, she stepped outside. No pastels here. Vivid bands of purple, magenta, and peach striped the sky. Bold colors, contrasting with each other, but making a perfect whole—like the man who increasingly occupied her thoughts.

The evening sounds of the desert broke the silence. The scuffling of a small animal burrowing into the ground, the caw of a crow, the shrill call of mating insects, each distinct, each necessary in the order of nature.

She let her mind wander, imagining she could hear another sound . . . the sound of Brad's voice reassuring the little boy as he clung to the horse. It was a sound she'd never forget.

The shopping trip into Billings proved a turning point for their relationship.

Jamie smiled, remembering how she and Brad had argued good-naturedly over whether Mrs. Milligan would prefer a new Sunday hat or a set of murder mysteries by her favorite author. They'd solved the problem by buying both plus a season ticket to the local baseball team's games.

Mrs. Milligan had been thrilled with the gifts. Jamie knew Brad had been more than a little embarrassed by the older woman's tears.

He'd hurried out of the kitchen with a mumbled excuse that he needed to check on Shakespeare.

Mrs. Milligan smiled indulgently. "He never could stand being thanked for anything. I think that's why he's always given me a check before. It kept everything impersonal." She patted Jamie's hand. "You're good for him."

Jamie flushed with pleasure but felt compelled to deny Mrs. Milligan's implication all the same. "Brad wanted to do this. I just went along for moral support."

"Oh, I know he wanted to do it," the housekeeper said. "But he's changed." She gave Jamie a shrewd look. "It doesn't take much figuring to know why."

"I'm afraid you're reading a lot more into this—"

Mrs. Milligan held up a hand. "I know I'm an old busybody, so you just tell me to mind my own business anytime I get out of line. But I know what I see and what I see is that my boy's done gone and found himself a sweet lady. And it's about time."

"Brad and I—"

But the older woman wasn't about to be sidetracked. "Did you know I've been with the family since that woman run off and left them?"

It didn't take a genius to know who "that woman" was, Jamie reflected.

"Brad's pa hired me a month after she'd gone. I guess by then he knew she wasn't coming back. Scott was just a baby. He was all right, but Brad . . . " The older woman shook her head. "He kept to himself mainly. Always was a good boy, tried to help with his baby brother, did a heap of chores, but he was a loner. I saw him cry only once—when his pa had to put down a horse with a broken leg. I held him and rocked him back and forth. After that, he never did shed a tear. Not even when his pa died. I think something died in him that day when his mama left him." She wiped her eyes with the corner of her apron.

Jamie felt tears prick her own eyes at the image of the lonely little boy.

The housekeeper bustled about, clearing away the wrapping paper. "Here I am just rattling on when you're probably anxious to be with your man."

"He's not my—"

"I'm glad he's got you now, honey. He needs you. Don't let him tell you otherwise. He pretends he doesn't need anyone, but you and I know different."

Jamie tried again to set her straight about the relationship between herself and Brad, but Mrs. Milligan only smiled and shook her head. "We'll see."

When Brad didn't come back to the house, Jamie wandered out to the barn. She found him there, using a curry comb on Shakespeare. Without a word, she picked up another and began grooming the horse's other side. They worked in companionable silence.

"Thanks for helping me choose a present," Brad said at last.

"I'm glad you asked me."

"I've never seen Mrs. Milligan cry over a gift."

"Maybe that's because she's never felt comfortable doing so . . . before."

"And she does now?"

Jamie nodded. "I think so."

He looked at her suspiciously. "What were you talking about with her?"

Jamie settled on part of the truth. "The past."

Brad scowled. "Why dredge up that? The past is dead and buried."

She leaned across Shakespeare and caught his hands. "Is it?"

"Of course it is."

But his voice lacked conviction. She heard it, the note of pain that Brad probably wasn't even aware of. Her heart ached for him, for the little boy who hadn't understood his mother's desertion and for the man who guarded his feelings so closely, afraid to let anyone close.

She knew better than to offer any sympathy, though. She had a feeling Brad wouldn't know what to do with it.

"I'd better be going," she said, sensing he wasn't going to let her get any closer, at least not today. "I've got a mountain of paperwork to do." She made a face.

His frown had faded, replaced by a grin. "I'll bet you like paperwork about as much as I do."

"If that means you hate it, then you'd be right."

He laughed, breaking the tension between them. "I'll take you home."

"Thanks."

Outside her house, he lingered, seemingly reluctant to leave. "It sounds like you could use a break from work. How about a ride tomorrow?"

"Great. I'll bring lunch."

Framing her face with his palms, he lowered his head to skim her lips with his own. "Tomorrow."

The word held a wealth of promise.

She worked her way through the reports that had to be filled out in triplicate, but her mind was far away. She couldn't forget Brad's discomfort with his housekeeper's tears. It had been more than simple masculine embarrassment over a woman's tears. He'd never learned to express emotion and was uneasy with others' expression of feelings.

Jamie reviewed what she'd learned today of his childhood and felt a surge of anger toward his parents, who'd denied him the security and love every child needed.

Maybe, just maybe, she could teach him that feelings didn't have to be feared. Brad had so much to give. If only she could convince him of it.

Chapter Four

Jamie found herself excited the following day. Whatever else happened, she would have this day with Brad. Nothing would spoil it, she promised herself. This would be their day, one for her to look back upon and cherish.

"Are you ready?" Brad asked, loosely tying Shakespeare's reins to the fence railing.

"Almost. I just wanted to give Mustard Seed an apple." Jamie handed the piece of fruit to the mare, who gobbled it down greedily.

"You spoil her," Brad said.

"I suppose you don't spoil Shakespeare?"

He laughed. "You got me."

As though aware that he was the topic of conversation, Shakespeare snorted and pranced about.

Brad patted the big gelding's neck. "I know, boy. You don't like to be kept waiting, do you?" He flashed Jamie a teasing smile. "That's what happens when you're taking a lady out, though."

She made a face at him.

Brad laughed. "Let me help you up." He checked

the length of the stirrups and, satisfied, gave her a boost up on Mustard Seed. He mounted Shakespeare, whispering to the stallion in a conspiratorial manner.

Jamie could have sworn the big gray nodded in agreement.

Brad kept the pace slow so that they could enjoy the scenery. Wildflowers cropped up in unexpected places, spots of brilliant color against the sun-seared ground. In spite of the drought, the land held its own kind of beauty, one filled with stark contrasts. The sky, as though to make up for the arid ground, was a vivid blue.

As though aware of her resolve that this be a day to remember, Brad proved to be an agreeable companion. By unspoken agreement, they avoided the topic of the mustangs. Today belonged to the two of them. There'd be time enough later to worry over the differences that separated them.

The sun bore down on them. Jamie swiped at the perspiration that trickled down her neck. When Brad suggested they stop for lunch at an outcropping of rocks, she was glad to comply. A flat overhang of rock provided a welcome bit of shade. Brad hobbled the horses while she opened her saddlebags and spread out the picnic lunch.

Brad looked at the array of food and whistled. "You've got enough here to feed an army."

"We could share with Shakespeare and Mustard Seed," she said.

"No way. They've got their own food."

She followed his gaze to where the horses chomped on the grain that Brad had brought for them.

Jamie poured lemonade from a thermos into paper cups and handed one to Brad.

He finished it in one gulp and held out his cup for more. "I didn't know anyone still made fresh-squeezed lemonade besides Mrs. Miller."

"I do. For special occasions." Jamie spoke without thinking and then wondered what Brad thought about her words.

He looked up but didn't say anything.

They feasted on fried chicken, deviled eggs, dill pickles, and chocolate chip cookies. By the time they'd finished, Brad was making a show of patting his stomach. "You keep feeding me like this and I'll get a paunch."

She looked at his flat stomach that boasted not a spare ounce of flesh. "Since you feel like you need the exercise, I'll let you clean up."

He gave her a pained look. "Thanks."

She stretched out, using her jacket to pillow her head, and watched as he repacked everything into the saddlebags. When he was satisfied that the area was spotless, he squatted down beside her.

He looked younger today, Jamie decided. More carefree. Maybe it was getting away from the ranch and all the responsibilities that went with it. She knew he loved what he did, but the work was backbreaking and never ending. He probably didn't take many days off.

"Do we have to leave right away?" she asked.

He had a pile of chores to do at the ranch, but one look at Jamie's face convinced him they could wait. For once.

"No. Not right away."

"Good."

He heard the satisfaction in her voice. She enjoyed being with him. The realization was a heady one. Most women wouldn't be content to spend the day under the scorching sun with nothing more exciting planned than looking at the scenery. But then, Jamie wasn't most women. He was beginning to accept that. It pleased him. It also scared him.

His contemplation was cut short with her next words.

"Tell me about your childhood. You never talk about it."

The air whooshed out of him. Whatever he'd expected, it wasn't this. He shifted so that he wasn't looking directly at her and stared up at the sky. Was that a cloud? Rain would be an answer to his prayers and those of the other ranchers.

He lowered his gaze and spotted a small lizard just as it scuttled out from underneath a rock. Just as quickly it took refuge under another one.

Jamie remained silent, as though sensing his need to think through his answer. He was grateful for the time. What did he feel about his parents after all these years? He'd like to be able to say that he didn't feel a thing. But that would be a lie.

He thought about all the years he'd felt driven to defend his mother, to downplay her desertion. With Jamie, though, he no longer felt compelled to gloss over the truth.

"My mother left when I was eight years old. She left. As in deserted. Abandoned." He laughed harshly. "She left her husband, her children, her home without a backward glance."

"But why?"

Brad heard the confusion in Jamie's voice and sighed, remembering. For a long time, he'd been equally confused. Closely on the heels of that came guilt. He'd blamed himself, wondering what he'd done to make his mother leave without so much as a good-bye. If he'd been more obedient, if he'd helped more with his new baby brother, if he'd been less trouble, would she have stayed?

The questions had tormented him for years until his grandfather had taken him aside and told him the truth. His mother had left her family because she was selfish. By then, Brad had convinced himself that he didn't care.

"My mother was a research scientist. She was good,

made a name for herself in microbiology, and published several papers.'' He stopped. ''Then she made the biggest mistake of her life.''

Jamie waited.

''She married my father and had children.''

He heard Jamie's quick intake of breath.

''She was never meant to be a wife or a mother. She didn't like ranch life. Said it stifled her. She left right after Scott was born.''

He kept his voice emotionless, but it didn't stop the tears from welling up in Jamie's eyes. He saw them and wished he had never started the story. But it was too late to stop.

''She teaches at Princeton now. She's happy.''

''How long has she been gone?''

''Twenty-five years.''

She reached out and covered his hand with her own. Her fingers wrapped around his, a wordless gesture of comfort that touched him more than he cared to admit. For long minutes, they stayed that way, neither feeling the need to speak.

At last, Brad pulled his hand away, breaking the spell. He heard Jamie's soft sigh of disappointment, but when he looked up her eyes were filled with compassion, not the censure he halfway expected.

''I'm sorry,'' she said. ''I'm sorry it hurt you so much.''

He started to deny that he'd been hurt and then

stopped himself. The simplicity of her words loosened the restraint he'd always felt whenever he talked about his mother.

"It was a long time ago."

She took his hand again. "Not that long."

She was right. He could still remember the bewilderment, pain, and guilt he'd felt that day when he returned home from school to find his mother gone. His father's gruff words had only added to Brad's confusion and hurt.

He supposed his father had tried. But he'd been too busy trying to care for a month-old baby to spend much time helping his eight-year-old son adjust to the loss of the boy's mother. Looking back now, he understood that his father was reeling from the shock just as Brad himself was.

"It was a long time ago," he said again, repeating the words in an attempt to comfort Jamie. He couldn't bear to see the distress in her eyes. "I'm a big boy now."

Her faint smile told him she understood what he was trying to do and appreciated it.

"What about your dad?"

Talking about his father was easier. Not by much. But enough to where Brad could remember the good times.

"Dad was a born-and-bred rancher. The ranch was his life until he started letting it go downhill. When he died, my grandfather ran it until I was old enough to take over."

"When was that?"

"When I graduated from college. I was twenty-one. My grandfather died shortly after that."

He lifted his head to stare at the wide expanse of prairie, as words from the past echoed through his mind. "Take care of the land and it'll take care of you," his grandfather used to say. Brad had listened. He'd built something his grandfather would be proud of.

Why then did he have such a gnawing sense of emptiness inside of him? He pushed the thought aside and turned his attention back to Jamie.

She looked at him with new understanding. "You took care of Scott and the ranch."

"He was pretty independent by then. It wasn't a big deal. I did what had to be done. Anyone would have done the same thing."

"Not anyone."

Brad didn't like the soft sympathy in her voice. He wasn't accustomed to sympathy, didn't know how to deal with it. He'd done what he had to. He hadn't thought about it; he'd simply done it. A man didn't look for praise for doing what had to be done.

"Enough about me. Tell me about you."

She lifted a shoulder. "You know most of it."

"I know what you told me. You put yourself through school and majored in biology."

"That's about it."

Brad knew all about going to school and working at the same time.

"It couldn't have been easy," he said, watching her face.

"No." She smiled. "Not easy. I knew what I wanted to do when I was five years old. I also knew I'd have to put myself through school."

"Couldn't your parents have helped you?"

"My parents were great. Dad was a mechanic. Mom taught school. There wasn't much money, but that never seemed to matter. We had a lot of love."

He knew a sharp pang of envy before pushing it aside. Love wasn't something he'd had a lot of experience with either. Oh, his physical needs had been met, all right, but love . . .

Even before she'd left, his mother hadn't had time for all the extra things a child needs and wants. Things like bedtime stories followed by a kiss to scare away the bogeyman, cookies and milk in the afternoon, a soft touch to bandage a skinned knee, a soft word to heal hurt feelings.

After his mother had gone, his father had turned to a bottle of whiskey and cards to find solace. And Brad and Scott had turned to each other.

Brad thought about some of the kids he'd met

through his weekend riding program and realized he'd been lucky. Even without parents, he'd had a brother, grandparents, and a home. Many of the kids he worked with didn't even have that much; they were wards of the state with no one to call their own.

He'd made it, but sometimes, in the dark hours before night slipped into day, he still wished for . . . He shook his head, impatient with the feelings that even twenty years hadn't been able to vanquish.

He found Jamie looking at him with warm compassion in her eyes, and flushed. The last thing he wanted was for someone to feel sorry for him, and he turned the conversation away from himself. "You grew up in the city? How'd you learn so much about horses?"

"I spent the summers with my grandfather. He worked on a ranch in southern California before moving here."

That explained a lot.

"I was a city girl before Grandpa put me on my first horse." She smiled. "I was only five, but I was hooked right then and there."

"A city girl, huh?"

"That's right. The closest I ever got to a horse was on television. Grandpa bought his land here the year I turned ten and invited me to spend the summer with him. When the end of August came, I didn't want to go home. I begged my parents to move here, but of course we couldn't."

"You loved your grandfather very much."

She nodded. "He died when I was sixteen. Even after all these years, I still miss him." Her voice stumbled over the lump in her throat. "I'm sorry. I'm not usually so emotional."

He pressed his hand over hers. "Love doesn't have a timetable."

"No, it doesn't, does it?"

He sensed she needed a change of subject and asked, "How long have you had this job?"

"Two years. The pay's lousy, my supervisor still thinks women belong in the kitchen, and there's always a pile of paperwork to do."

"But you love it."

She smiled softly. "Yeah. I love it."

"It sounds like you're making your dream come true."

"Everyone needs a dream. What's yours?"

Brad hesitated. He'd never discussed his dream with anyone. Not even Scott. "Making the ranch a paying proposition. Right now, it's self-supporting, but only just."

"There's more, isn't there?"

"There's more. But it's not likely to happen so there's no point in discussing it."

She took his hand. "There is if you want to make it come true." At his disbelieving look, she said, "You have to say the dream out loud. At least twenty times a day. That way, you start believing it can happen.''

Still, he remained silent.

''Tell me. Please.''

He'd never put words to his dream before. Not even to himself. The idea scared him, but it tugged at him as well. He suddenly wanted to say the words aloud, to test them. He looked at Jamie and knew there was no one else with whom he'd rather share his dream.

''I want to turn the ranch into a place for children with disabilities. Full time.''

She drew in a deep breath. Whatever she'd expected, it wasn't this. But then, she wasn't really surprised when she'd had a moment to think about it. She'd seen how much Brad cared about the children who spent the weekends at his ranch.

''It'd take money,'' he said with a long sigh. ''Lots of money. More than I could put together for a long time the way things are going right now.''

''What would you need to start making the kind of money you'd need?''

''We'd have to breed more mares, plus buy a couple more stallions.''

She was beginning to understand his anger over the loss of his mares to Conquistador. It wasn't the money that Conquistador had cost him, but the mustang had robbed Brad of his chance to realize his dream.

''I wish you'd told me sooner,'' she murmured.

"What difference would it have made?"

"None, I'm afraid. But at least I'd have understood." She uncurled her hand from his and cupped his face. "It's a wonderful dream, Brad. You'll make it come true. I know you will."

He smiled. "You're a born optimist."

"No. I'm just someone who believes that dreams can come true. If you want something enough, you'll make it happen."

He wanted to believe her. He wanted it more than he could remember wanting anything. But life had taught him some hard lessons, ones he wasn't likely to forget.

They were quiet now. It was a good kind of silence. The kind that gave a person room to think . . . to feel. Jamie didn't fill it with chatter. She was easy to be with. Right now, she was content to simply be.

He looked down at her and smiled. Her eyes were closed, her face tilted up to catch the sun. She didn't have a smidgin of makeup on, her hair was windblown, she wore faded jeans and a shirt that had seen better days . . . and she was the most beautiful woman he'd ever known.

He took her hand and turned it over. Her nails were short and unpolished, her skin red and work-roughened. "You can tell a lot about a person by her hands."

"What are you? A palm reader?"

"Uh-uh. A man who knows hard work when he sees it." He stroked the faint ridges of calluses along her palms. "And feels it."

"My work takes me outside most of the time." She eased her hand from his.

He saw her flush and guessed at its cause. "Don't be embarrassed. Your hands tell me you care about what you do."

"But you don't approve of what I do."

"It's not a question of approving or disapproving. I respect someone who fights for what he—or she—believes in."

"Like you?"

He laughed shortly. "Yeah. Like me."

Brad lifted his head, looked at her trembling lips, and pulled away. His breathing was not quite steady as he picked up an apple.

Were he and Jamie alike?

At one time he'd have denied it emphatically. But now he wasn't so sure. She was committed to her job. So was he. She fought for what she believed. So did he. She loved the land. So did he.

The list went on until he was shaking his head. She'd found a way through the defenses he'd built. But that didn't mean that he felt anything more for her than the ordinary attraction that a man feels for an attractive woman.

She was more than attractive. She was also bright,

intelligent, and articulate. She challenged him, making him think and question things. No other woman had ever affected him that way.

"Dreaming?" she teased, ending his air of abstraction.

He cast an uneasy look at the sky. "I don't much like the look of those clouds. We'd better start back." He began packing up the remains of their lunch.

She shook crumbs from the blanket and folded it before handing it to him.

He tucked it in his saddlebags and gave her a leg up.

"Thanks," she said and swung her leg over the saddle.

The ride home held none of the morning's easy camaraderie as the stillness in the air grew. Jamie was beginning to feel sore and held herself stiffly erect on Mustard Seed. The horse's motion, which had earlier felt like a gentle swaying, now became a jarring ride as Brad pushed them faster.

He must have seen the lines of pain on her face, for he pulled Shakespeare to a halt. "We can stop for a few minutes."

She tried not to grimace as she dismounted, but she couldn't hold back a gasp of pain. Strong hands closed around her waist and helped her down. She rested against a boulder while Brad tethered the horses.

Lightning flashed through the sky, a prelude to the

heavens opening up in a downpour. Jamie lifted her face to catch the sweet taste of rain upon her lips. *The end of the drought*. She turned to smile at Brad, but her smile died when she saw the anxious glances he darted at the sky.

"What's wrong?"

"Nothing, I hope. Come on. Let's get out of here."

Thunder rumbled around them as lightning splintered the sky. The rain, which had been only a gentle patter before, now beat down harshly on them.

Brad started to unhitch the horses. He'd just finished with Mustard Seed when thunder rolled through the sky. The big gelding reared back, his hooves slicing the air.

"Whoa, boy," Brad shouted. "It's only thunder. Nothing to get excited about."

The horse pawed the air, and Brad sidestepped, barely missing being struck by Shakespeare's hooves.

Jamie rushed to help Brad.

"Watch out," he cried when she got too close.

Shakespeare, now thoroughly spooked by the bursts of thunder and streaks of lightning, struck out again. Brad took a running leap, pushing Jamie out of the way just as the horse's hooves hit the ground.

Winded, they sprawled on the ground as the rain pummeled them.

"Thanks," she said as she managed to sit up, wiping mud from her face.

"No problem." He pulled himself up and groaned.

"What's the matter?"

"My leg." He ran his hands down his leg and winced when he reached his ankle. "I must have sprained it when I fell."

"You mean when you pushed me out of the way."

"It doesn't matter how it happened. Help me over to Shakespeare."

With her help, Brad hobbled over to where Shakespeare waited skittishly. He pranced to one side as Brad came closer.

"It's all right, boy," Brad crooned, reaching for the reins.

Just as he finished speaking, a flash of lightning splintered the sky.

Chapter Five

Shakespeare jerked away. Trying to stop him, Brad caught hold of the rope coiled on the saddle, stumbled, and fell heavily.

Jamie grabbed for the reins, but the big horse reared back sharply, evading her grasp. She edged closer. "Easy. It's all right."

Again, she reached for the reins, but Shakespeare had bolted, disappearing into the grayness of the rain, with Mustard Seed close behind him.

She started after them.

"Don't bother," Brad called after her. "They're long gone."

She blinked against the rain. "Will they find their way back home?"

"They'll be all right." Brad laughed shortly. "I'm not so sure about us."

She rushed to help him as he tried to get to his feet. He tried to shake off her arm.

"Don't be stupid," she said. "Your ankle . . . does it hurt a lot?"

"I've had worse."

"That's not what I asked."

He grimaced. "Yeah. It hurts." White lines of pain were etched around his mouth. His breath came in short, sharp gasps that even the rain couldn't drown out.

"It's my fault," she said. "If I hadn't—"

He touched her lips with his finger. "It's no one's fault." He winced as he sank back down on the log.

She knelt beside him, heedless of the mud. "I didn't think."

"Hey, no more of that. I'll live."

The rain pelted them mercilessly, and she huddled deeper into her jacket. "Is there some kind of shelter around here? An abandoned cabin? Anything?"

"There's an old outrider's cabin about two miles downstream." He shielded his eyes against the rain. "You can make it if you follow the river."

"*We* can make it," she said.

"Jamie, I'm not going anywhere." He patted his leg. "Not with this ankle. If it's not broken, it's sprained close enough not to matter."

"You can if you lean on me."

"I outweigh you by at least seventy pounds."

"So?"

He gave her an impatient look. "You'll never be able to take my weight."

"Let me decide what I can take. Now, are you going to sit around whining or are we going to get going?"

His eyes narrowed. "Whining?"

She held his gaze with a level one of her own. "That's what I said."

Slowly he shook his head. "You're one heck of a woman, Jamie Freeman."

"Save the flattery, and give me your hand." He slipped his hand inside hers, and she helped him up. "Now, put your arm over my shoulders."

Brad did as she said. She winced as part of his weight shifted onto her. Her legs buckled. Only his quick reflexes kept them from landing facedown on the ground.

"This isn't going to work," he growled.

"I just need a minute to get used to it." She braced her legs and straightened. "Okay."

She slid her arm around his waist. "Let's get going."

They made their way cautiously, picking their way over the uneven ground. As the rain grew heavier, they slowed their pace even more. Rivulets began to wend themselves over the unabsorbent land. Water collected in depressions in the earth.

When Jamie slipped in a muddy spot, Brad caught her, but the effort cost him. She could feel it as his body tensed against hers.

By mutual consent, they stopped in the shelter of some bushes. "This is crazy," he said between breaths. "You can't keep it up much longer. You've got to leave me and go for help."

She brushed her hair back from her face. "If the positions were reversed, would you leave me?"

"No. But that's . . . "

"Different?" She had to shout to be heard over the howl of the wind and rain.

"Yeah."

"How's it different? Because I'm a woman?"

"This is getting us nowhere, Jamie. I'm not trying to put you down. You've got more guts than anyone I know. But we've got to face facts. We've been at this for over an hour, and we've barely covered a half mile."

"And we'll cover the next half and the next and the—"

"Anybody ever tell you you're one stubborn woman?"

"Yeah. I seem to remember someone saying that to me. Turns out he was right."

For the first time in an hour, he grinned. "You win."

"Good. Because I'm a poor loser."

"I'll remember that."

She stood and then reached down to help him up. She knew what it cost him to accept her help and understood. She had her own share of pride. "C'mon. I've always wanted to see what an outrider's cabin looks like."

He grunted as he got to his feet.

For the next hour, they didn't talk. Jamie was grateful for the silence. She needed every bit of energy she could muster to put one foot in front of the other.

The rain pummeled them until they could barely see beyond the next step. She concentrated on keeping her footing as the ground grew more slippery by the moment. She couldn't afford to fall—she might not make it back up again. They continued to follow the river until Brad held up a hand.

"The river narrows somewhere around here," he said, speaking for the first time in an hour. "It's probably our best chance of crossing it."

She looked at the swollen river. The water churned around the rocks, spilling over the banks in some places. "Are you sure?"

He followed her gaze. "As sure as I can be."

She helped him sit down against a rock where an overhang provided a bit of shelter. "Let me look around, see if there's any place that looks better." She returned a few minutes later, trying not to let her worry show. "You were right," she said with determined cheerfulness. "Looks like this is as good as it gets."

Brad pushed himself up and uncoiled the rope he'd slung over his shoulder. "Here," he said, handing it to her. "Tie it around your waist." When she'd finished, he did the same, linking them together. "I knew this'd come in handy."

Their arms around each other, they eased off the bank and stepped onto the sand that bordered the river. Their feet sank immediately.

Jamie hesitated. ''Maybe—''

''C'mon,'' Brad shouted. ''It's not going to get any better.'' He tightened his hold, and they plunged into the river.

She gasped as the icy water whipped around her legs. With Brad leaning heavily on her, she scrambled for footing and nearly went under. Only the rope chaining them together saved her. She paused to catch her breath.

''We can't stop,'' he yelled above the roar of the water.

She understood what he meant. Already she could feel her feet and legs begin to grow numb. It wouldn't take many minutes in the water before they lost feeling altogether.

She and Brad slipped and slid their way toward the far bank. The water rose higher until it lapped around her chest. For each step forward, they were pushed back two. The rope gnawed into her waist.

Then she saw it.

The surging water had loosened a boulder headed straight toward them.

She started to shout a warning, but one look at Brad's face told her he'd already seen it. Their movements hampered by the raging current and the rope tying them together, they dodged to one side, barely missing it.

"Whew," she gasped, realizing how close they'd come to disaster. A blow from the rock could have stunned them—or worse.

At last, they neared the bank.

"We made it!" Jamie cried. "We made it!"

"Not quite," Brad said. He pointed to the boulders that stood like sentinels guarding the riverbank.

She didn't need to be any closer to know they were too high and too slick to climb. She could barely keep her footing as it was. There was no way she could climb over the rocks.

She gulped down her dismay. "We'll make it."

Before she finished speaking, strong hands caught her around her waist and thrust her forward until she was atop one of the smaller boulders. Even over the bawl of the water and wind, she caught the grunt of effort it cost him to boost her up. Where he found that last burst of energy, she didn't know. He had to be at least as exhausted as she was.

She scrambled to an upright position. Her feet found purchase on the rock, and she turned to help Brad. "What are you doing?" She watched as he started to unfasten the rope from his waist.

He ignored her and struggled with the knot, his efforts hindered by the cold rain and his own numbed fingers.

She knew what was going to happen if he succeeded in freeing himself. "No," she shouted.

"It's the only way. I'll be all right."

He was lying. They both knew it. She'd made it out of the river only because Brad had shoved her onto the rock. There was no one to help him.

No one but her.

"I won't let you," she yelled.

She yanked on the rope, deliberately twisting herself away from him so that he couldn't destroy the last link between them. For once the cold and rain worked for her as his fingers fumbled in trying to untie the rope. He couldn't do it. They were bound together, and she didn't intend severing that tie.

"Let it go, Jamie," he yelled, still yanking at the knot.

"You're not getting rid of me that easily. Now, grab it and hold on."

Muttering something under his breath, he grasped the rope.

Bracing her feet against the boulder, she began to pull. She ignored the pain as the rope bit into her waist; she ignored the burning of the hemp against her palms and the rain and wind that battered her. She ignored everything but pulling Brad to safety.

The river lapped at the rocks, further hampering her efforts as she slid on the slick face of the boulder.

"Let go!" Brad shouted over the bellow of the wind. "You're not strong enough."

She didn't waste her breath answering but continued pulling. The rope bit deeper into her palms, and she spared a moment to regret the loss of her gloves.

For every inch gained, they lost two as the river dragged him back again and again. Blowing rain stung her face while the wind buffeted her back and forth. Exhaustion was making her arms heavy; her breathing was labored. She knew it was taking its toll on Brad too as he fought being swept away by the water.

"Let go," he said hoarsely.

She strained to catch his next words.

"It's no use."

"You let go, and I'll come in after you."

He must have believed her, for he kept hold of the rope.

She measured their progress in fractions of an inch. She didn't think about how much farther they had to go; if she did, she was afraid she'd give up. The distance separating them grew smaller, imperceptibly at first, then more noticeably. The knowledge that they were winning fueled her strength, and she redoubled her efforts.

Just when it looked as though they'd made it, Brad fell backward, the pull on the rope dragging her over the boulder. She clawed for something—anything—to grab onto. At last her fingers found a jagged edge of rock. She held on and prayed.

She felt the rope gnaw at her waist as Brad struggled to stand up. If she didn't move quickly, they'd both be pulled into the river. She forced herself to her feet and managed to flash him a smile before she started pulling again.

It could have been minutes—it seemed like hours—before Brad crawled over the rock. He lay there, panting heavily. She slumped down beside him, her breath coming in ragged gasps that threatened to turn into sobs. She made a conscious effort to slow her breathing.

"Lady, you're something else," he said.

"Thanks. I think." She wanted to give way to the weariness that hovered only a breath away, but she pushed herself to her feet and offered Brad a hand. Together, they negotiated the slippery surface of the rock and made their way to the river bank. "We're going to make it."

"Thanks to you."

It was too dark to see his smile, but she could hear it in his voice. She reached for his hand and found her own caught in his strong grip. Only then did she remember the rope that still bound them together. They fumbled with it until at last Brad managed to undo the knots.

They spared a few minutes to catch their breath

before starting on their way. The struggle in the river had cost them both, and Jamie knew she couldn't go much farther. A glance at Brad's face, drawn tight with fatigue and pain, confirmed that he was in even worse shape.

Her wet clothing clung to her, chilling her all the way through. If they didn't get warm and dry soon, they were in danger of hypothermia. Even in the summer, hypothermia could prove fatal. They trudged over the ground until she caught sight of something. She clenched his arm.

"I can see it. I can see the cabin!"

Minutes later, they shoved open the door and stumbled inside. The cabin was dirty and rough and smelled of stale smoke. And she'd never seen anything look so good in her life. She sank onto the only cot.

"How does a fire sound?" Brad asked.

"Heavenly." She stood. Her stiff, sore body groaned its protest against moving so soon. "I'll—"

Gently he pushed her back down. "You've done enough. I'll start the fire."

Within minutes, a small blaze filled the stone fireplace. Jamie edged closer, basking in the warmth, and rubbed her arms together. She turned her back to it, feeling like a marshmallow that's been toasted on both sides. She stayed there until the heat became too much. Her jeans and shirt were stiff and encrusted with mud, but at least they were now dry.

"Here," he said, handing a blanket to her. "Wrap this around you."

She accepted it gratefully. "Thanks."

It smelled like everything else in the cabin—musty and stale. But it felt wonderful, and she pulled it tighter around her. The coarse material chafed her hands where the rope had cut into them, but she didn't mind. Right now, she was too grateful to be alive.

"How long do you think we'll have to stay here?" she asked.

"Until morning. When we don't make it back, Scott will send out a search party. Don't worry," he said and tucked a wet strand of hair behind her ear. "They'll find us."

"I'm not worried," she said softly and discovered it was true. She and Brad were both safe. Nothing else mattered.

"Good." He rummaged through a rough-hewn cabinet and pulled out a can of peaches. He pried open the lid with a knife he found in a drawer and passed the can to her. "Dinner."

She winced as her hands closed around the can. Rope burns scored her palms. Fortunately, Brad had turned away for a moment and hadn't noticed. She fished out a peach half with her fingers and popped it into her mouth. "Mmm." She sighed in appreciation. "I didn't know canned peaches could taste so delicious."

They shared the peaches and then drained the can

of the syrup. Her stomach grumbled, and Jamie placed her hand over it, hoping Brad hadn't heard.

A look at his face told her that he had. "There's one more can of peaches," he said. "Shall we have it now or save it for later?"

Her stomach rumbled once more, deciding the issue. When they finished eating, they licked the peach juice from their fingers.

Brad glanced around. "I'm sorry we're stuck here."

"I'm not."

He looked at her curiously.

"I'm just glad we're alive and out of the rain. All that water was starting to make me shrivel up."

They laughed together, breaking the tension.

He stabbed his fingers through his wet hair, drawing her attention to the gash that grazed his cheek.

"Let me have a look at it," she said.

"It's nothing." But he didn't object when she pressed her kerchief to it.

She rummaged through another drawer and pulled out some gauze and tape. "This place comes equipped with its own first-aid kit."

"It's standard practice for people to leave supplies behind for the next person."

She busied herself bandaging the gash and hoped he didn't notice her hands. They were shaking by the time she'd finished. She supposed that reaction was setting in after their ordeal . . . or was it reaction to Brad's nearness? Right now, she didn't feel like deciding which.

"Thanks," Brad said, rubbing his arms together.

"You're shivering." She pulled the blanket away from her and handed it to him.

"You keep it."

"We'll share."

Their backs braced against the side of the bed, and the blanket draped around their shoulders, they sat cross-legged in front of the fireplace.

"You saved my life back there," he said quietly.

Jamie drew in a deep breath. "I did what anyone would have done."

"Not anyone. You could have let go, let me take my chances in the river. No one would have blamed you."

"I would," she said softly.

He gave a half-turn so that they faced each other. "I know. You're as stubborn as those mustangs you're trying so hard to save."

"And you're not?"

"No way. I'm just an easygoing kind of guy."

Their laughter mingled, a reassuring sound after the last harrowing hours.

She watched the play of light and shadow as firelight spilled over his face, turning his skin to bronze and emphasizing the whiteness of the bandage. His hair, rain-dampened and dark, fell across his forehead. Shyly she reached up to push it back.

He tucked her under his arm so that her head rested on his shoulder. "Thank you, Jamie," he said, his voice hoarse. "I'll never forget what you did."

"You shoved me up on the rock. If you hadn't—" She shuddered, knowing she couldn't have made it on her own.

"Let's call it even," he said.

"Even," she murmured.

The fire's snapping and sputtering merged with the rain's staccato beat on the roof in a comforting rhythm. The warmth of Brad's arms invited her to snuggle deeper. She fought the drowsiness that wrapped itself around her, beckoning to her to give in to it. She'd close her eyes for a moment . . . only a moment . . . until the wave of exhaustion passed.

Brad listened as her breathing slowed. Her lashes formed crescent-shaped shadows across her cheekbones. Her lips parted, she looked soft and vulnerable in sleep. He touched his lips to hers and prepared to wait out the night.

His body clamored for sleep, but he knew he couldn't afford the luxury. He had to watch the fire; even more, he had to check on the river. If it rose anymore, they'd have to leave the cabin.

Right now, he wasn't sure if he had the strength to stand up, much less hike to higher ground. His body felt battered and bruised; his ankle ached with a dull throb. He reminded himself it could have been worse—a lot worse—if Jamie hadn't pulled him out of the river.

He shifted positions and stretched the kinks from his arm. Thunder rumbled while rain continued to pepper the roof. Carefully lowering Jamie to the floor, he pulled himself up and grimaced as his ankle threatened to give way. He hobbled over to the window and peered out. Seconds later, he heaved a sigh of relief. There was no sign yet of the river flooding its banks. Maybe they'd get lucky.

He stumbled back to where he'd left Jamie asleep on the floor. Slipping an arm under her knees and the other around her shoulders, he picked her up, laid her on the bed, and smoothed the blanket over her—no sense in their both spending a night on the hard floor.

He resumed his position in front of the fire, but it wasn't the crackling flames that warmed him. Memories of the last few hours swirled around in his brain. He couldn't forget how Jamie had risked her life to save his own. He'd meant it when he said that no one, including him, would have blamed her for letting go of the rope. But she'd held on to it and pulled him out of the river.

How she'd done it, he'd never know. He outweighed her by at least seventy pounds; the river had fought her every inch of the way, yet she'd refused to give up.

She'd hung on with a grim determination that not even the force of the raging water could defeat.

He pictured her as she'd been perched on the rock, hair whipping around her face, eyes sparkling with anger when he'd ordered her to let go. His lips twitched as he remembered how she'd threatened to come in after him if he severed the rope that bound them together. He didn't doubt she'd have done exactly that.

She'd been scared. He'd seen it in her eyes, heard it in her voice. Only a fool wouldn't have been frightened given the fix they were in. But she hadn't given in to her fears. She'd fought her way through them, saving both of them.

She stirred restlessly, tossing the blanket off her. Automatically, he reached to tuck it back around her. It was then that he saw her hands. Dried blood had caked on her palms, which were covered with angry red scrapes. It didn't take much figuring to know what had caused them: rope burns she'd sustained while saving his life. He'd been too busy trying to hang on to the rope to remember what hemp could do to unprotected skin. Gently he lifted one of her hands and brought it to his lips. He pressed a kiss to her fingertips before tucking her hand back under the blanket.

He remembered how she'd looped the rope around her waist. Her shirt would be scant protection against the constant rubbing of the rough edge of the rope as she used her own weight as leverage.

He watched as she turned on her side, fitting her fist under her chin. She looked hardly older than a child at that moment, her face scrubbed clean by the rain, her hair falling in damp curls around her face. He brushed one back from her cheek, his hand lingering there for a moment. Her skin was soft, flushed from the heat of the fire. He traced the smattering of freckles sprinkled across her nose.

He touched his cheeks, surprised to find them wet. He wasn't accustomed to tears, especially his own. But they fell freely now. He didn't bother to wipe them away as he thought of how her hands must have been on fire as she pulled him to safety. He remembered how she'd kept them hidden from him, obviously wanting to spare him from knowing about the pain she'd endured while saving his life.

Outside of Scott and his grandfather, no one had ever cared that much about him, putting his needs above their own. The knowledge warmed him even as it humbled him.

For once, he let his emotions have free rein.

He cared about Jamie. It didn't make sense trying to deny it any longer. He'd fought that attraction and his growing feelings for her. Only now was he willing to admit that it was a losing battle.

For over twenty-five years, he'd refused to acknowledge the pain his mother had inflicted on him by her desertion. He'd grown so adept at hiding his feelings that he'd managed to fool everyone, including himself. Jamie had penetrated the wall he'd erected around himself.

The only question was, what was he going to do about it.

Chapter Six

She awoke slowly, her limbs stiff, her head achy. Memory came back just as slowly.

The storm . . . Brad's injury . . . crossing the river . . . She pressed her fingers to her temples to relieve the pain lodged there. Thin sunlight trickled through the dirt-streaked windows, but it was enough to tell her that the rain had stopped.

Somehow she'd ended up on the cot. Brad must have put her there last night after she'd fallen asleep. She didn't remember anything beyond sitting in front of the fire.

She pushed away the blanket that covered her and winced as her hands closed upon the coarse material. A glance at her palms had her quickly looking away.

"I see you've finally decided to join the living."

She looked up to find Brad watching her. "I think so." Cautiously, she sat up.

"Are you all right?" he asked, crossing the room to sit beside her.

She was stiff and sore and longed for a hot bath,

but she was alive. "A little the worse for wear. What about you?"

"I'll live," he said.

She raised her eyebrows at the brusqueness of his voice.

"Jamie, let me see your hands."

She understood then. A man like Brad wouldn't easily accept that someone had been hurt while saving his life. Automatically she folded her hands in her lap. "What for?"

He gave her a level look. "Why didn't you tell me that you'd hurt them?"

"I didn't want you to worry." She saw the self-reproach in his eyes. "They'll be all right."

"Let me have a look. Please," he said when she still hesitated.

Reluctantly she held out her hands.

Brad turned them over gently. He flinched at the scrapes and abrasions, which looked even worse in the light. "These must hurt like—"

"They hardly hurt at all. Really," she added when she saw that he didn't believe her. "They look worse than they are."

He fitted a finger under her chin. "You're a rotten liar. I'll bet your waist hurts even more."

Her eyes gave her away. "Some."

He opened the first-aid kit and pulled out some bandages. ''You should have told me,'' he said as he bent over her hands.

He was so close that she could feel his warm breath. Stubble darkened his jaw, and she wondered what it would feel like if she reached out and touched it.

After he finished applying the bandages, he walked away, still favoring his right leg.

Sighing, she pushed herself up and started after him. ''Brad?''

He didn't turn around.

She placed a hand on his shoulder and felt a shudder go through him. ''It wasn't your fault. It wasn't anyone's fault. It just happened.''

He spun around. ''I should have been the one taking care of you. Not the other way around.''

''You did. You pushed me up that rock. Besides,'' she said, barely able to hide her exasperation at his masculine logic. ''I thought we'd gone all through this last night.''

''That was before—''

''Before what?''

''Before I saw your hands.'' His lips compressed in a tight line.

Her annoyance grew as she realized he was angry. She bit back sharp words when understanding hit her. He was angry, all right. But not with her. He was angry with himself.

''It doesn't change what you did. You saved my life

when you pushed me up those rocks.'' She reached up and kissed him, a soft brush of her lips against his. She drew back, more than a little surprised at her boldness.

Brad slipped an arm around her waist.

Involuntarily she winced, and he released her. ''I'm sorry. I forgot—''

''It's all right.''

''When we get back, you're seeing a doctor.''

''Speaking of getting back . . . '' She stopped, listening.

''I think that's our rescue now.'' He hobbled to the window and rubbed his sleeve against the grime. ''It's Scott and some men from the ranch.''

She moved too quickly and groaned. Brad was right. Her waist did hurt where the rope had burned her. She ignored the pain and joined him as he went to open the door.

''About time you got here,'' Brad said as Scott bounded up the porch steps.

Scott looked from Brad to Jamie. ''We had to wait until daylight before setting out. Are you two all right?''

''We're fine,'' Brad said.

Jamie watched as the brothers hugged each other. Brad had no problem expressing his feelings for Scott. Why couldn't he share what he felt for her? She had no time to brood over the answer as Scott bombarded them with questions.

''What happened to you two? When Shakespeare and Mustard Seed came home without you, I figured they'd gotten spooked in the storm.''

''Are they all right?'' Brad asked.

''Not a scratch on them,'' Scott said. ''I rubbed them down myself. They spent the night in a nice dry barn.''

''How'd you know where to find us?'' Jamie asked.

Scott grinned. ''This is the only shelter in miles. I figured Brad would head here.'' His smile died. ''You two sure you're all right?''

''We're fine,'' Brad answered for both of them. ''Thanks to Jamie.''

Scott quirked an eyebrow.

''I'll explain later,'' Brad said, his bad leg giving way as he turned around.

Scott slid an arm around Brad's shoulder. ''What'd you do to yourself?''

''Let's just say I've had better days.'' He flashed a smile at Jamie. ''How 'bout you?''

''Much better,'' she agreed. Inwardly, though, she couldn't help thinking that having this time with Brad was worth everything she'd been through.

''Thought you two might be hungry,'' Scott said, handing a paper sack to Jamie.

As if on cue, her stomach growled, causing the men to laugh. She was too hungry to be embarrassed and joined them even as she opened the bag. Inside she found biscuits sandwiched with thick pieces of ham. She and Brad devoured the food, not bothering to talk until they'd put away two sandwiches apiece and washed them down with a thermos of coffee.

"You're a lifesaver," she said to Scott when she finished.

"I owe you one, little brother," Brad said.

"I'll remind of you that later," Scott said. "Right now, let's get you home."

Scott helped Brad mount a brown gelding, then turned to Jamie. "We'll get you home," he promised as he helped her mount a beige mare. "It just may not be soon. The rain's washed out a lot of trails."

"How're your hands?" Brad asked Jamie in a low voice. "Will you be able to ride?"

"I told you they don't hurt," she said, but already she was having doubts about being able to grip the reins.

To her relief, he let the matter drop.

The ride home was long and slow as they took several detours to avoid washed-out trails and flooded areas. The landscape had changed overnight under nature's caprice. Flowers burned brightly under the sun against newly carved ridges in the ground.

"It's never the same, is it?" she asked.

Brad shook his head. "And yet always the same."

She understood what he meant. The land, always

changing and yet ever the same, drew them together even as it pulled them apart. She feared their differences over the mustangs would always separate them, but for now, she was content to enjoy the harmony between them.

She felt the same closeness she experienced last night, that sense of having shared something important. Her body was bruised and sore, her hands raw and bleeding, but she'd have gone through it all again for this one moment with Brad. She wanted to tell him, even started to, but was stopped as Scott pulled up alongside her. Brad sketched a wave and joined the other two riders.

"I was plenty worried when your horses returned without you," Scott said.

"I'm just glad you found us."

"So am I. What'd Brad mean back there when he said 'Thanks to Jamie.' "

She shrugged, uncomfortable with the turn of the conversation. "He was just talking. I think his leg's hurting him."

Scott gave her a long look. "You don't have to tell me if you don't want to. But don't tell me that Brad was 'just talking.' Brad never says anything he doesn't mean."

"It's just that—"

"She doesn't want to own up to saving my life," Brad finished for her, pulling up on her other side.

"Maybe she's having second thoughts about it now." But the smile on his lips belied his words.

"We had trouble crossing the river," Jamie said. "I helped him out of it. He'd have done the same for me."

Scott gave a low whistle. "You pulled Brad out of the river? A little thing like you?"

She raised her chin. "I did what I had to."

"She sure did," Brad seconded. "I wouldn't be here if she hadn't."

"You're a hero," Scott said.

"Heroine," Brad corrected.

She flushed. "Could we drop it? Please."

The men exchanged glances with each other.

"Sure," Brad said.

Her embarrassment faded as she struggled to keep hold of the reins with her injured hands. They'd started bleeding again, and no amount of blotting them with the sleeve of her shirt would stanch it.

"How much longer is it?" she asked Scott, trying to make the question casual.

"An hour. Maybe a little more."

"An hour?" She couldn't quite keep the dismay from her voice.

They'd reached a particularly rough piece of ground, and the steady motion of the horse's pace became a jarring bounce. Automatically her hands tightened on the reins. She couldn't bite back her groan in time.

"What is it?" Brad asked, his face creased with concern.

"Nothing."

He pulled up on the reins of his horse and leaned over to her, gently prying her hands free from their grip. His lips tightened into a thin line as he looked at her hands. He looped an arm around her waist and lifted her from her horse to set her in front of him. He gestured for Scott to take the reins.

"Jamie's riding with me. Don't try to hold on," he said to her. "Just lean back and let me do the work." His arms closed around her, enveloping her in their warmth.

She wanted to tell him she could make it on her own, but the pain in her hands convinced her she'd be lying. "All right."

"All right?"

"You expected an argument?"

She felt his nod behind her.

"Sorry to disappoint you."

"I'm not disappointed, sweetheart. Just surprised. And relieved." His voice sobered. "Why didn't you tell me your hands had started bleeding again?"

"I didn't want—"

"You didn't want me to worry. It's too late. I'm already worried. Don't you know your hands could get infected?"

"What was I supposed to do about it? Whine and cry that they hurt? What good would that have done?"

"You'd never whine."

The simple words warmed her more than could any effusive praise or flattery. She didn't question why a few words from Brad meant so much. She was very much afraid that she already knew the answer. The realization caused her to stiffen in his arms.

"Relax," he said.

She did as he instructed and leaned against him, feeling his arm tighten around her waist. The rhythm of the horse's gait soon lulled her into a light sleep.

When she awoke, Brad was reining in the gelding at the barn.

"We're home," he said and handed her down to Scott.

"I can walk," she protested but was quickly overruled as Brad dismounted.

"For right now, let me take care of you." He took her from Scott and started toward the house.

"Your leg—"

"My leg will be fine. Right now, it's you I'm worried about."

The concern in his voice warmed her even as she warned herself not to read anything more into it than what it was. He carried her through the kitchen and down a hallway. When he started toward the stairs, she tugged on his arm.

"I can make it on my own. If you try carrying me up those stairs, you'll hurt your leg even more."

She could sense the debate going on inside him. Finally, he released her and set her on her feet. She took a steadying breath. Brad kept his hands at her waist, looking as if he wanted to say something. The moment passed, and Jamie suppressed a sigh of regret.

Brad showed her into a bedroom and disappeared, only to return a few minutes later with some clothes. "I borrowed these from Mrs. Milligan. They won't fit, but they'll do until you get home." He paused. "The doctor will be here in a while."

"A doctor who makes house calls?"

"Jim Franckum's an old friend. Besides, he owes me a favor."

Gratefully, she peeled off her clothes, now stiff with dried mud, and stepped into the shower, careful to keep her hands away from the spray. The hot water felt wonderful against her skin. She shampooed her hair twice before she was satisfied she'd removed the last of the river water and mud from it.

Regretfully she stepped out of the shower and dried off. She slipped into the clothes Brad had provided, looked at her reflection in the mirror, and laughed. She'd never win any awards for glamour in this getup. The voluminous dress swallowed her whole. She cinched the belt around her waist. As she opened the door, she caught the aroma of bacon frying.

She followed the delicious smell into the kitchen where she found Brad talking to Scott. He stopped in midsentence when he saw her. She knew he was trying hard not to laugh, but the crinkles at the corners of his eyes gave him away.

"Go ahead and laugh," she said.

His laughter sent a skitter down her spine. He was so attractive when he forgot to be wary around her. Scott joined in, but she couldn't tear her attention away from Brad, entranced as she was by the warmth in his eyes.

"You don't look so bad," Scott said after several minutes. He negated his words when a chuckle slipped out.

"You look beautiful," Brad said softly. The laughter had died from his eyes, but the warmth remained, a warmth that had her longing to touch her lips to his.

For a moment, she forgot that Scott was there, Mrs. Milligan was in the next room, and the doctor was due to arrive any minute. She forgot everything but Brad and how he was looking at her. She swayed toward him and only remembered where she was when he gestured to the table.

"Dr. Franckum'll be here in a few minutes," he said. "In the meantime, we can have breakfast."

Only now did she recall the tantalizing aromas that had drawn her to the kitchen in the first place. Her stomach growled, and she pressed a hand to it.

Scott laughed. "I'll see you two later. Someone's got to do some work around here." He ducked as Brad threw a dish towel at him.

"Hey, little brother," Brad called as Scott headed outside. "Thanks again."

Scott flashed a grin to include them both. "You're welcome."

Brad held out a chair for her.

"How's your leg?" she asked.

"Sore. What about your hands?"

"Sore."

They traded smiles, but she couldn't help feeling self-conscious. The feeling persisted while they ate breakfast. When the doctor arrived, Jamie was more uncomfortable than ever even though she'd changed back into her own clothes, now washed and dried.

"How'd you do this?" the doctor asked as he applied salve and bandages to her hands.

She felt Brad's gaze on her. "Rope burn," she said, hoping he'd let it go at that.

"Jamie pulled me out of the river," Brad said, his eyes not leaving her face. "She saved my life."

"I just did what you'd have done for me." She lifted her face to smile at him, but the closed expression in his eyes caused her to draw back.

Jamie sighed.

He had withdrawn from her as effectively as if he'd built a wall between them.

Chapter Seven

She wasn't surprised. Not really. But she was disappointed. After all they'd been through, he'd pulled back into himself with no hint remaining of the man who'd opened up with her, sharing his dreams, his fears.

"You'd better let me take a look at your waist," the doctor said, drawing her attention away from Brad.

In the bedroom she'd used to change clothes earlier, Jim Franckum gave a low whistle as he examined her waist. The skin was raw and tender where the rope had cut into it. "You must have felt like your skin was on fire," he said as he applied the salve.

She forced a smile to her lips. "I didn't notice it at the time."

He gave her a long look. "No. I guess not," he said, handing her several tubes of salve. "Use this until it's all gone."

"Thanks, Doctor."

Once he'd looked at Brad's leg and said it was badly sprained but nothing more, she knew there was no reason to stay any longer. "I guess I'd better be going."

Brad stood. "I'll take you home."

Was he so eager to be rid of her, she wondered? She was saved from answering when the doctor offered to give her a ride.

"I'll be happy to run you home," he said. "You ought to stay off that leg, Brad."

Brad looked ready to object when Mrs. Milligan laid a hand on his shoulder. "I'll be making sure he obeys orders, Doctor."

Jim Franckum kept up a running commentary during the ride home. He didn't seem to expect her to add much, for which she was grateful. Her thoughts kept returning to Brad and how he'd shut her out.

"You're thinking about Brad," Jim said as he pulled his car in front of her house.

She turned to him, startled. Was she so obvious?

The doctor smiled. "I've known Brad for over twenty years. He's a good man."

"I know," she said quietly.

"Don't let him push you away."

She remembered Mrs. Milligan using the same words. "Why does he do it?"

"Self-preservation."

"I'd never hurt him." As soon as she said the words, she wished them back. She'd all but told the doctor that she loved Brad. The sympathy in his eyes, though, convinced her he'd never betray her confidence.

Jim patted her hand. "I think he knows that. But he's been hurt in the past. Badly. Be patient with him."

"Thanks, Doctor," she said, letting herself out of the car. "For everything."

"Take care of those hands," he reminded her.

"I will. And thanks again." She waved good-bye.

Two hours later, she switched off her computer and pushed her chair back from the desk. She'd intended spending the day compiling her findings and typing her reports, but her mind refused to cooperate. Crossing the room, she looked out the window, trying to focus on the dazzling light the sun cast on the tin roof of the work shed. It too failed to hold her attention.

She rationalized her inability to concentrate with the thought of her injured hands. They *had* begun to throb, but she knew it was more than the pain that kept intruding on her work. It was something much more elemental and far more disturbing . . . the memory of Brad's withdrawal from her.

It had been deliberate. Perhaps that was what hurt the most, the realization that he knew what he was doing and felt compelled to do it anyhow.

She shouldn't care, but it was too late for that. Far too late. Like it or not, she cared about Brad. She was beginning to believe that she always would. And now that caring was perilously close to loving.

Once more, she stared out the window, seeking something—anything—to tear her thoughts away from him. Deciding to survey the effects of the storm, she headed outside. She stepped gingerly around pockets of muddy water that dotted the rough ground. The sun shimmered over the rain-washed fences and barn.

It was beautiful. The land never failed to arouse a strong feeling of connectedness within her. She'd felt it years ago when she'd come here as a child. The feeling had lain dormant for the last ten years, but now it tugged at her, reminding her that this was her home. When her job tagging the mustangs was over, she intended to remain here. If the Society didn't have any work for her, she'd find another job. Anything that allowed her to remain here.

That settled, she smiled for the first time since she'd left Brad that morning.

Brad silently cursed his injured leg. If not for that, he'd have been on Shakespeare, riding, feeling the wind whip through his hair, instead of stuck behind a desk with his leg propped up on a stool. Not that he was accomplishing much, he acknowledged ruefully.

He'd stared at the same set of figures for the last hour without making any progress in sorting them out. He rubbed his jaw, his fingers encountering the graze along his cheek. Memories of Jamie bandaging it caused him to pause.

She'd been gentle, as he'd known she would, her touch as soft as her voice. He frowned, remembering his reaction to that touch. Jamie had found her way past the barriers he'd kept firmly in place for over two decades. She'd done it simply by being herself.

"You've got it bad, man," he muttered to himself, remembering how he'd just about bitten Scott's head off when his brother commented that he and Jamie seemed to be getting along well.

He had no right taking out his frustration on Scott. The simple truth was that he was afraid. Afraid of what Jamie was doing to him. He was also more than a little attracted to her. But that was it. It had to be. There was no room in his life for a woman, except on a friendship basis.

He didn't intend to trade that in for the heartache of marriage. Hadn't his parents taught him anything?

He swore softly.

No, he didn't intend getting caught in that trap. Only, why did he feel so empty now? As if he were letting something precious slip away?

He forced his attention back to the monthly report. The ranch was operating in the black—by a healthy margin. If he could only keep it that way for the next few months, he'd be in good shape for the winter. But no matter how he juggled the figures, there was no way he could afford to hire a foreman to manage the ranch. If he could, then he'd be able to devote more time to investigating opening up the ranch full time for children with disabilities.

He knew Scott would drop out of law school if he asked him to stay on and help run the ranch, but he couldn't—he wouldn't—destroy his brother's dream for the sake of his own. Scott had planned on being a lawyer since he was in grade school. Another year and he'd be ready to take the bar.

Brad kept at it for another hour, paying bills and balancing the books. At last, he shoved his chair back and stood. The hours of inactivity had stiffened his leg, and he grimaced as he pushed himself to his feet. Maybe a short walk outside would ease the soreness. He opened the French doors leading to the patio. A few minutes in the fresh air . . . The thought went unfinished as Mrs. Milligan poked her head in the room.

"Mr. Brad, you heard what the doctor said," she said, hands on her hips. "You're to take it easy."

He sighed. "I was just going for a walk to stretch my legs."

"And you'll be paying for it tomorrow." She folded her arms across her ample bosom and waited.

She was right. He knew it. What's more, she knew he knew it.

He lowered himself back into the chair.

She smiled approvingly at him. "Would you like your dinner in here? Mr. Scott's out for the evening."

He was about to say he wasn't hungry, when he

thought better of it. Mrs. Milligan was only taking care of him in the best way she knew how. He couldn't disappoint her. "Thanks. I'd like that."

"Good. You just rest that leg. I'll be back in a minute with your dinner. I made your favorite—pot roast with new potatoes, carrots, and onions."

Brad watched as she bustled out of the room, his gaze softening. She was the closest thing to a mother he'd ever had. She'd helped him with his homework, tended him when he was sick, and scolded him when he'd deserved it. He smiled, thinking she wasn't above giving him a scolding even now when she thought he needed it.

He'd urged her for years to stop working so hard, but she'd only shaken her head and told him her job was taking care of him and Scott. Once Brad married, she'd said more than once, then she'd consider taking it easier. He'd never had the heart to tell her that marriage wasn't in the future for him.

Unbidden, pictures of Jamie intruded into his thoughts. She'd make a good wife and mother, he decided. She had the right blend of softness and strength, compassion and humor to cope with the demands of raising a family. He had no doubt that when she committed herself, it would be forever.

Impatiently he pushed the thought away. He had no right thinking of Jamie in those terms. No right at all.

Then why did it feel so *right?*

* * *

"Miz Freeman, I warned you. I warned Brad. Now it's gone and happened. I hope you're satisfied."

Jamie stared at Nate Henderson in bewilderment. The rancher, astride a black gelding, loomed over her menacingly. "What happened, Mr. Henderson?" She held her ground.

"That rogue made off with six of my best mares. Came down out of the hills last night and stole 'em right out of the pasture." He jabbed a finger at her. "This is your doing, Missy. If you hadn't been so all fired set on saving that thievin' rogue, I wouldn't be out six mares."

"I'm sorry, Mr. Henderson. Sorrier than I can say."

"Sorry ain't gonna pay the freight. I'm gonna make sure you lose your job."

She gasped. "You're not serious."

"You bet your britches I'm serious. Dead serious." He eyed her shrewdly. "You'd best git while the gittin's good."

She lifted her chin. "I don't run from trouble."

"Trouble's what you got, Missy. In spades."

Brad had warned her what might happen, but she had been too stubborn to listen. She looked up at the rancher, trying to find a spark of understanding in his eyes that she could appeal to. "Mr. Henderson—"

"Those mares were my living. You cost me a passel of money. Whaddya plan on doing about it?" He shot her a look of such righteous indignation that she flinched.

"I'm terribly sorry. If I can do anything—"

"You're darn right you can. You can get rid of those rejects from a glue factory."

"But it wasn't—"

Henderson was already stomping away. "You heard me, Missy," he called back over his shoulder. He climbed astride the horse and glowered down at her. "You got no business being here. No business a'tall."

Jamie watched him ride away. *He won't go through with it. He can't hold me responsible.* But even as she said the words, she knew she was lying to herself. Brad had warned her. So had Scott. Still, she'd refused to listen.

Shoulders drooping, she followed the path from the garden to the corral where six horses pranced and whinnied.

How could such beautiful creatures arouse so much hatred? She stood there for long minutes, trying to decide what she should do. The burning rays of the late afternoon sun persuaded her to head back to the house. She turned to retrace her steps, only to be confronted by the sight of another rider.

Brad.

The familiar figure dismounted and strode toward her. The set of his shoulders and the grim lines bracketing his mouth boded trouble. Gone was the man with whom she'd survived a harrowing experience. His eyes, once so warm, were cold and accusing now.

The cut on his cheek had healed. She wanted to trace the barely visible scar, as if by doing so she could bring back the feelings they'd shared such a short time ago. Could it be only a few days earlier that she'd felt closer to him than she had to anyone in a very long time? Deliberately she kept her hands at her sides.

She knew a cowardly impulse to run. Instead, she stood her ground.

"Jamie."

"Brad."

She took the initiative. "You heard about Mr. Henderson's horses."

"The whole county's heard by now." He pushed a hand through his hair. "I was afraid this would happen. Why didn't you listen?"

Stung at his tone and lack of understanding, Jamie lashed out, her anger cutting through the apology she had been about to make. "What about the mustangs? Don't they have rights?"

"Henderson may go under with the loss of those mares. He was depending on them for next year's breeding. He's not some rich guy playing at being a rancher. He's like the rest of us—just someone trying to make a living at the only thing he knows how."

This time, she refused to meet his gaze. "I'll find his mares. I'll start tomorrow. I told Mr. Henderson I was sorry. I don't know what else to do.'' Her anger spent, she bowed her head. ''I never meant to hurt anyone.''

Brad's gaze softened at the sight of her downturned head, but she didn't see it. She scuffed her boot toe at the tufts of prairie grass that dotted the ground.

''Look, Jamie, I know you didn't mean for it to happen. I'm on my way over to Henderson's now to see what I can do.'' He wanted to take her in his arms, to kiss away the hurt and confusion that clouded her eyes. With an effort, he kept his hands at his sides. ''I'll try to smooth things over with him. He's not a vindictive man. I think I can get him to see reason—if we can find his mares.''

All at once Jamie was weary. She didn't need another problem. And she didn't need—or want—charity from Brad or Henderson either. ''Don't bother on my account,'' she snapped. ''It's my problem, and I'll handle it.''

''Like you've already done.'' He wanted to retract the words as soon as he'd said them, as soon as he saw the trembling of her lips, but she'd provoked him beyond reason. *Why couldn't life ever be simple*, he wondered. He reached out a conciliatory hand toward her, but she ignored it. ''I'll talk with him, see if I can calm him down,'' he repeated. When she didn't answer, he muttered, ''I'll be seeing you.'' He turned and left.

Jamie stared after him, wanting to call him back and tell him she was sorry. He'd only come over to help, and she had thrown it back in his face. All for the sake of pride.

She trudged back to the house. She had to think, to find a way out of this mess. But the only thing she could remember was the coldness in Brad's eyes as he'd looked at her.

"Think of it, Brad," Nate Henderson said. The beefy rancher leaned back in a leather chair, puffing on a cigar. "We could attract hunters from all over. Make it a real big shindig. It'd bring a lot of tourist dollars into Dream's End." He dragged deeply on the cigar. "If it goes well, we can do it again next year."

Brad hesitated, recoiling from the idea of a mustang hunt. But he could see Nate's point. The town needed a boost. In the last year, six stores had closed their doors and shut down. Did he have the right to deny local merchants the chance to make the much-needed money that an event like this could generate?

"There's got to be a better way," he said at last, thinking of his own idea and knowing now wasn't the time to air it. "Besides, what makes you think people are going to go for a mustang hunt? Most people are squeamish about shooting horses, no matter how big a nuisance they are."

Henderson stood, hooked his thumbs in his jeans

pockets, and rocked back on his heels. "You weren't around when we had trouble with the devils back in the thirties and forties. We put a bounty on them. All a man had to do was bring in the ears."

Brad grimaced, but the older man ignored it.

"We'll divvy up the money we need for bounties between all the ranchers. They won't mind coughing up some money to get rid of that black devil and his band of marauders."

Brad didn't bother to hide his distaste for the scheme.

"Appears to me you ain't giving this a chance," Henderson grumbled. "Folks like a chance to get together—don't matter what the cause. We could even sell tickets. Families can bring picnic lunches. I bet every hotel room in town would be filled. Not like now. Poor 'ol Ed Flannery at the hotel can't fill even half his rooms. He told me something's going to have to give, or he'll be out of business before the end of the year."

Brad nodded reluctantly. Ed had told him the same thing.

"What do you have against killing off some mustangs?" the other man demanded. "You gone soft all of a sudden?"

"You know me better than that."

Henderson snorted. "Appears maybe I don't. I figured you as one of us. Now you're sounding like one of those bleeding hearts." He gave Brad a sly look.

" 'Course, maybe it's not you that's talking. Maybe it's that female. What's the matter? You so gone on her you can't talk for yourself anymore?"

Brad's mouth hardened.

Henderson jabbed a finger in the air. "She ain't one of us. She don't belong here. Never will."

"Maybe you'd better shut your mouth, before we both forget that we're friends."

"I ain't so sure about that anymore." Henderson jammed his hat on his head. "I ain't so sure about that a'tall." Without a backward glance, he strode out.

Brad stared after him, more troubled than he cared to admit. Nate Henderson blew a lot of hot air, but this time, Brad was afraid, he was serious. Dead serious. And his talk with Henderson had only stirred the rancher up further.

A mustang hunt with bounties offered was bound to attract a lot of attention, both good and bad. He couldn't like the idea. Everything in him revolted against it. But neither could he dismiss it when Conquistador was robbing the ranchers of their best stock. An injection of cash into the town wouldn't hurt either. Henderson was right about that.

Brad slumped at his desk. He'd been friends with the older man for over ten years, but their friendship had been tested today when Henderson had started in on Jamie. Brad had been sorely tried not to put his fist through Nate's face.

His thoughts slipped back to Jamie. She'd be madder than a wet hen if she caught wind of a mustang hunt. And she wouldn't be shy about telling him so either.

His lips curved into a reluctant smile. That was one of the things he liked best about her. She wasn't afraid to say what she meant. Just as she wasn't afraid to stand up for what she believed in, no matter how unpopular the view.

His smile died.

He didn't want her hurt. She'd become special to him. He didn't delude himself into believing that there was anything more than friendship between them—he wouldn't let there be. He'd learned his lessons too well from his parents.

Jamie hadn't meant to eavesdrop at the feed and grain store two days later. She'd only stopped in to buy a few supplies, but she couldn't ignore the loud voices that filled the small space.

"Did you hear Henderson's organizing a mustang roundup? There's gonna be a bounty on 'em. All a body's got to do is bring in the ears and collect a hundred dollars. A cool hundred for a pair of ears."

She stole a peek to see who was talking. A paunchy, bald man in jeans, plaid shirt, and scuffed boots leaned against a counter, talking to the store owner.

"I hear he's gonna advertise a reward for the man who brings in the most," the owner put in.

"It ought to help all of us, not just the ranchers." The rancher gave the other man a knowing look. "Won't hurt you none either. All those cowboys itching to make a fast buck. Not to mention the tourists."

"You can bet I'm laying in a stock of ammunition. Don't normally carry the stuff, but this could be big. Real big."

The bald man shook his head admiringly. "You've got to hand it to Nate and Brad. I think they're really onto something."

"What's Brad got to do with it?"

"You kidding? Brad's as anxious to get rid of those bandits as the rest of us. They've given him plenty of grief too. Stole three of his best mares last month."

Jamie remained where she was, afraid if she moved, she'd give herself away. She couldn't face anyone—not now, not when it seemed her world was falling apart. She held on to the hope that it was all a big mistake. Brad wouldn't be involved in anything like that. He couldn't be.

"You sure about that?" the store owner asked. "That don't sound like Brad. He's always had a soft spot for the mustangs, 'specially that black stallion."

She waited. Hoping. Praying.

The rancher pushed back his hat and glared at the clerk. "Sure I'm sure. I got it straight from Henderson. Brad may have a soft spot, but he ain't gone soft in the head. Least ways, not yet." He laughed.

She swallowed past the lump lodged in her throat and waited until their backs were turned before slipping out the door.

At home, she tried to muster some enthusiasm for the ham salad she'd fixed herself, but the food tasted flat and dry. She pushed it away and headed out to the barn. It needed mucking out, and she needed an outlet for her feelings.

Two hours later, covered with bits of straw and smelling strongly of "country sunshine," she put down the pitchfork and surveyed her efforts. The barn had never looked cleaner, which was a lot more than could be said for her, she thought with a grimace of distaste.

But the activity had accomplished its purpose. She was too tired to think, too tired to worry, too tired to do anything but take a shower and fall into bed.

She awoke the next morning with sore muscles and a heavy heart. She'd promised Nate Henderson she'd find his mares, and she wasn't going to accomplish that moping around feeling sorry for herself.

Ten hours later, she was ready to admit defeat. She'd managed to catch a glimpse of the mustangs, but she'd never gotten close enough to see if Henderson's mares were with the herd or not.

The next day met with the same success, and she returned home weary, both in body and spirit. Whether she liked it or not, she needed help.

The only trouble, she acknowledged grimly, was that

the only person she could have turned to was the same person she had been avoiding. Two days later, she drove to Dream's End. A stop at the hardware store brought her face-to-face with the last person she wanted to see.

"Jamie, we have to talk," Brad said, taking her arm.

"What about?"

Brad glanced about the crowded store, where curious eyes took in their every move. "I'd rather not do it here. Have lunch with me?"

She owed him that much. A tiny hope flickered in her heart. Maybe it was all a mistake. She would ask him about the mustang hunt, he would deny his part in it, and . . .

She let him steer her to the same restaurant where he'd taken her only a few weeks ago. It seemed like more. When they were seated at a secluded booth at the back, Brad ordered. The waiter reappeared shortly, bearing plates of steaming ribs.

She waited.

Brad took her hand in his, ignoring her attempts to pull it away. "Look, I know you're upset about Henderson and the mustangs. That's what I want to talk to you about."

Please, let him say he had nothing to do with it. Please.

"Nate and I have been talking . . ."

So it was true. Her breath deserted her in a whoosh. She picked up a fork, toying with it as she tried to think of a way to excuse herself as quickly as possible.

"I think we can—"

"Did you talk with him about putting a bounty on mustangs?" she interrupted.

"I went to see Nate about his mares," Brad said, his tone cautious, eyes wary. "I told you that."

"Did you discuss it or not?"

Brad sighed, knowing he had no choice but to answer. "Yes, we did, but it wasn't the way you think."

Jamie stood, preparing to leave.

He grabbed her hand, pulling her back down. "If you'll give me a chance to explain—"

"I don't need to hear anything you've got to say. I knew we didn't see things exactly the same way, but . . . " She swiped angrily at the tears that gathered in her eyes.

Brad saw the tears, wanted to kiss them away, and knew he'd probably get slapped for his trouble.

"I didn't believe it. Not even when I heard it the fifth time. Everyone's so excited, you'd think it was Christmas, instead of mass murder."

"It's hardly murder."

"Oh. What would you call it? A bunch of hunters with their high-powered rifles shooting at defenseless animals?"

"You're not trying to understand the other side,"

Brad said, beginning to get riled. "This could mean a lot of money to businesses that might otherwise go under."

"And that's what counts, isn't it?" she asked contemptuously. "Money."

"You bet it counts. Businesses close up, people go hungry without it."

He gripped her shoulders, urging her closer across the table. His nearness threatened to shatter her composure. A day's growth of beard shadowed his face. The masculine scent of him tantalized her nostrils, further sidetracking her from her purpose.

She knew he was right and that she was being unfair. Still, she couldn't condone what he and Nate Henderson were planning.

"I don't want to fight with you about this," Brad said. "But neither can I turn my back on people who've been my friends for years. They think this could be good for the town as well as making the land safer for our stock. I won't tell them not to try. I can't."

She shook off his hands. "I'm sorry, Brad. I know you have to do what you think is right. But so do I." She stood once more. This time he didn't try to stop her.

Jamie walked out of the café, her head high. No one looking at her would know of the pain that wrapped itself around her heart.

At home, she flipped through the newspaper listlessly, trying to decide what she should do. An item on the editorial page caught her attention. Readers were invited to write their feelings about the proposed mustang hunt.

Two hours later, she looked over the paper she had just pulled from the computer. It was good, she decided. At least she hoped so. Before she could change her mind, she folded the letter into thirds, sealed it in an envelope, and dropped it into the mailbox.

A week later, Jamie opened the newspaper to the editorial page with a mixture of anticipation and dread. It was there. The paper had printed the entire letter. She drew a sharp breath as she read it. It sounded so much more vehement now than it had when she'd written it. A tremor of fear skittered down her spine. What would Brad think of it?

Chapter Eight

The pulse at the base of his throat quickened its beat as Brad read and then reread the column. *What the heck does she think she's doing?* " . . . the mass murder of innocent animals indicts those proponents of the . . ." His lips tightened.

A knock at the door interrupted his thoughts.

"Brad, did you see—" Scott held the paper in front of him.

"Darn right I saw it," Brad growled. He grabbed his hat and stood.

"Where are you going?"

"Where do you think?"

"Maybe you'd better wait till you cool down."

"I don't want to cool down. What I *want*—"

"Brad, wait."

He gave his brother an impatient look. "What?"

"Jamie has a right to her opinion. Just because it doesn't agree with yours doesn't mean it isn't valid."

"Don't start practicing your lawyering on me. I'm not in the mood."

Scott stood his ground. "Well, maybe you'd better be."

"I suppose you agree with her. Do you think I'm some kind of murderer too?"

"Of course I don't. But I don't agree with a mustang hunt either."

"Neither do I." Brad started to the door. "Don't wait up for me."

The peremptory knock at the door could belong to no one else but Brad. Jamie thought of ignoring it and decided she couldn't put it off. When she opened the door, he looked so grim and forbidding that she involuntarily took a step backward.

He didn't wait for an invitation and walked inside, slamming the door behind him.

Feeling the need to have her hands occupied as well as to keep a distance between herself and Brad, she went back to the kitchen and resumed washing dishes.

His lips tightened at her obvious ploy as he followed her.

"Why? Why did you do it, Jamie?" He waved the paper at her, folded at the page of her editorial. "It makes us sound like a bunch of bloodthirsty sadists."

"I'm sorry you see it that way. I only wrote what was happening. If you and your friends don't like it—"

"Don't like it? Every animal protection agency in the state will pounce on this."

"I'm sorry," she repeated. "But I can't stand by and watch you and Henderson stage a slaughter without trying to do something about it."

"Maybe there won't be a slaughter," he said. "If you'd only given me some time—"

"To do what?"

"To find a way out of this. Now, you've gotten Nate and the others so mad, they'll never back down."

"What makes you think they'd back down anyway?"

"There's a chance. There *was* a chance," he corrected himself. "Do you think I want this? Do you?" His hands cupped her shoulders.

Surprised by his intensity, she looked at him. "I don't know, Brad. I thought I did. One time. But now . . . I just don't know."

His anger spent, he dropped his hands. "I didn't want a mustang hunt, and not just because of you. I've never hunted. Never wanted to. This . . . " He waved his hands, then dropped them in defeat. "If you'd only waited. I was working on something that might have stopped it. What's the use?" His shoulders drooped tiredly.

Exhaustion had deepened the fine lines that fanned outward from his eyes and furrowed grooves around his mouth. Her gaze softened.

Brad gathered her to him, his arms closing around her. His mouth sought hers, finding there the sweetness that could, if he let it, block out everything else. It was so simple when they were like this.

Knowing he was losing his objectivity, he drew back.

She felt the loss of his arms around her. Even more, she felt his withdrawal from her. She drew a deep breath. "I'm sorry," she whispered. "I wish things were different."

"So do I," he murmured, drawing her to him once more. He rested his chin on the top of her head. "So do I." He resisted the temptation to kiss her one more time. "I have to go. Maybe I can still do something about this mess."

Bemused, she stood staring at the door, seeing not it but the tall, infinitely disturbing man who held her heart. She wanted to call him back, to promise anything if he would only stay.

Gravel and dust spat from beneath the tires as he pulled out of the driveway. He'd handled it badly. He knew it. He could still see the pain in Jamie's eyes. But what was he to do? He couldn't turn his back on his friends, but neither did he want to go through with a mustang hunt. Every fiber inside of him revolted at the idea. There had to be another way.

There had to be.

Three hours later, he pushed back his chair, smiling.

He didn't have all the details figured out yet, but he was convinced his plan would work. Once he worked out the snags, he'd take it to Henderson and the rest. He'd make them see reason.

It was so simple he wondered why he hadn't thought of it before. A meadow, virtually unusable because of its isolation, occupied the northernmost tip of his property. His lips quirked as he recalled the story of how his father had won it forty years ago in a poker game with a friend. Bordered by a rocky ridge, it was sheltered from the worst of the elements and fed by an underground spring—a perfect home for the mustangs.

He did some quick calculations. It just might work. A half smile erased the tired lines that had furrowed his forehead moments ago. He searched through a sheaf of land and soil surveys. A report he remembered filing over a year ago netted him the information he needed.

His excitement grew by the moment. A roundup could still be held, attracting tourists and bringing business to Dream's End. Moving the mustangs to higher ground, where they couldn't threaten the ranchers' stock, should satisfy Henderson and the others. Now, if he could only get Jamie to agree to the idea.

She'd still want to tag the mustangs, but he could help with that. His pulse quickened at the thought that they'd be working together. It would give them a chance to work toward a goal rather than against each other.

Brad found that his own feelings about the mustangs had changed. Several months ago, he'd have been eager to rid the land of what he considered nuisances. Now, seeing the problem through Jamie's eyes, he understood her commitment to preserving the wild horses.

He expelled a sigh and then frowned, wondering when this had become so important to him. It had nothing to do with his feelings for Jamie, he assured himself.

Nothing at all.

Conquistador had calmed down considerably since Brad and Scott had brought him in, but Jamie wasn't fooled by the stallion's docile behavior. For now, it was enough that he was here, safe.

If it hadn't been for Brad . . . She shook her head, refusing to contemplate what might have happened—what probably would have happened—if he hadn't convinced Nate Henderson and the rest to drop the idea of the mustang hunt. Instead, Brad and Scott had captured Conquistador and a dozen other mustangs and brought them to Jamie.

It was up to her now to tag the stallion. Then Brad would take him and his herd to the high meadow. There, with the natural shelter provided by the ridge rimming the area, they'd be safe. What's more, they'd no longer be a threat to the ranchers.

When she'd asked who owned the meadow, he'd brushed aside her question and reminded her of the work still ahead of them. She'd dropped the subject but not her interest. A trip to the town hall of records confirmed what she'd already suspected: Brad owned the land.

She hadn't been surprised. She'd already known that Brad cared more about the mustangs than he cared to admit. But to give up part of his ranch as a refuge spoke more eloquently than words of his concern for the wild horses.

She smiled, thinking he'd never be one for pretty words and speeches. He was a man who did what had to be done without fanfare. It was one of the things that had first attracted her to him.

Her smile dissolved as she acknowledged one area she wished he'd give voice to—his feelings for her. She knew he cared for her. She even dared hope that caring had grown into love. But he'd never used the word. In fact, he seemed to avoid it deliberately.

Her lips tightened as she thought about the reason behind his refusal to admit his love.

His mother had left him a legacy of distrust and fear. Jamie's heart ached for the lonely little boy who blamed himself for his mother's desertion and his father's withdrawal. An eight-year-old child shouldn't have to carry that kind of burden. If only he'd let her get close enough, she knew she could teach him that love didn't have to end in pain.

She'd felt the subtle shift in their relationship as they'd worked alongside each other the last week tagging the mustangs. When he'd invited her to his place on the weekend to help with the riding program, he'd been as carefree and happy as one of the children. But the following day, he'd slipped back behind a mask of distant politeness.

Holding back a sigh, she headed to the house. Monthly reports were due in a few days' time. The never-ending paperwork was a constant annoyance, taking her away from the horses she loved. Two hours later, she rotated her shoulders in an effort to relieve the tension knotted between them. Crossing the room to look out the window, she gasped.

Black clouds scuttled across the sky while the wind swirled dirt and gravel over the yard. She'd been so engrossed in her work that she hadn't even heard the ruckus outside. She hurried to the door. It swung crazily on its hinges as she pushed it open. Not bothering to grab a coat, she headed to the corral, shielding her eyes against the sting of sand as it whipped around her.

Conquistador would go crazy penned in the corral during a bad storm. He was a wild creature, accustomed to the freedom of open spaces. She had to release him before he hurt himself trying to escape.

Thunder roared over the squall of the wind, ricocheting off the mountains and canyon walls. Not to be outdone, the wind picked up even more, blustering its way across the ranch yard. Almost blinded by the blowing sand and dirt, she groped for the latch to the corral. Something sharp pricked her fingers. It was then she realized the gate was broken.

She was too late.

Conquistador had already freed himself. She looked closely and saw the splintered wood that littered the ground, mute evidence of his strength. She walked farther into the corral and peered through the whirling sand, but she couldn't make out the mustang. He was probably long gone. She knew it was for the best. They'd find him again and . . .

A low whickering alerted her that she wasn't alone. She turned slowly. Conquistador, black as the night that surrounded them, had approached so silently she hadn't heard him.

He was less then ten feet from her, his nostrils flared, his head lifted. The storm had spooked him. She saw the fear in his eyes, fear rapidly turning to fury.

She stood her ground, knowing any show of fear on her part could be fatal. "Good boy," she said, her voice low and soothing. "No one's going to hurt you."

A rolling snort ripped from his nostrils as he pawed the ground.

She backed up a step, hoping she could ease out of

his way before he directed his anger toward her. Too late she realized she'd backed herself against the railing. One foot at a time, she edged to the side, all the while keeping up a soft stream of comforting words.

"Everything's all right. It's only a storm. You've been in storms before." She inched her way to the broken gate. If she made it there, she could make a run for the barn. "You don't want to hurt me. I'm your friend."

Conquistador stopped and pricked his ears. She didn't hear anything but the hammering of her own heart. Ironically, its pulsing beat reminded her of hooves pounding the ground. He must have heard something, for he went very still.

But she wasn't deceived. He was poised to strike, his hooves as lethal as razor-edged clubs. She continued her retreat, her steps infinitesimal. The distance to the gate was slowly diminishing, but she knew a hopeless feeling when she measured it against the speed with which the stallion could attack.

Plumes of dust enveloped them, and she resisted the urge to swipe at the dirt that coated her lips. Any movement could enrage the mustang. She couldn't risk it. A few more feet and she'd be home free. One step. Two. Only another foot.

A flash of lightning spooked him, and he reared back. She moved at the same time. For a moment, she thought she'd made it. Her hand closed over the fence post. She gripped it and started to back out when the blow came.

She saw it coming—the huge hooves slicing through the air. Instinctively she ducked, but it was too late.

She was falling. Falling. Falling.

Pain splintered through her, and then there was nothing. Only blackness, an inky blackness that swallowed her into its chasm. For a second, only a fragment of a second, that time before she relinquished herself to the comfort of the nothingness that beckoned as a respite from the pain, she was reminded of Conquistador's coat.

"Scott, hold down the fort. I'm going over to Jamie's place. I want to check on the mustangs."

Scott grinned. "Sure."

Something in Scott's tone bothered him. "What's that supposed to mean?"

"And checking on the mustangs is the only reason you're going?"

"What else is there?"

"It's as plain as the nose on your face. You love her. And she loves you."

Brad paused. "What makes you think that?"

"I've seen how she looks at you." Scott dropped an arm around his brother's shoulders. "And I've seen how you look at her. You love the lady. The only one who doesn't know it is you."

Brad didn't bother correcting his brother. He wasn't in love with Jamie. Sure, he cared about her. He respected her. He even liked her. But love? No way. He wasn't about to get caught in that trap. Love wasn't in the cards for him. It never had been.

He was frowning as he drove to her house. Scott didn't know what he was talking about. He was dating a girl now, someone special, according to him. Obviously his own romance was causing him to see something between Jamie and Brad that wasn't there.

Still, Brad couldn't deny that he was looking forward to seeing Jamie. Now that they'd resolved their differences about the mustangs, they could enjoy each other's company without fighting. That was it, he thought in relief. He thought of her as a friend. A man could never have too many friends. That settled, he relaxed; a smile tugged at his lips at the thought of spending the evening with Jamie.

Lightning zigzagged through the sky, and he drove a bit faster. If the storm spooked the mustangs, Jamie could have more than she could handle. His smile died as he parked in front of her house and climbed out of the truck. The wind had stirred up the dust, making visibility practically nil.

Something was wrong.

He didn't know how he knew. It was more a feeling, a gut reaction he'd learned not to ignore. He scanned the yard and corrals. Everything looked normal, but he couldn't shake the feeling that caused his neck hairs to stand at attention. Lights blazed inside the house. Telling himself to relax, he strode up the stairs to knock on the door. When there was no answer, he pushed it open.

"Jamie?" He listened, willing her to answer.

Pushing open the door, he walked through the small living room into the kitchen. A computer sat on the table with the cursor blinking. Knowing it was useless, he searched the rest of the house. Nothing appeared out of order. It only heightened his feeling that something was terribly wrong.

He pushed open the door and headed out to the barn. Perhaps she'd gone to check on one of the horses . . . and left the computer on? She could have forgotten it.

There was no reason for his growing anxiety, no reason except for the feeling in his gut that told him to hurry. He didn't waste time looking around the yard. Every instinct urged him toward the barn.

It was quiet.

The wind had suddenly ceased, and an eerie silence took its place. There should have been something. He knew Conquistador was in the corral. The mustang was probably going out of his mind with panic at being confined during a storm.

Maybe Jamie had already released him. That was it, Brad told himself. She'd gone outside to check on the horses and decided to let the mustang go before the horse hurt himself. Then why hadn't she heard his arrival? He pushed away the question. The pricking at the nape of his neck made a mockery of his attempt to convince himself that everything was all right.

He let his eyes adjust to the darkness. Fear clawed through him as he saw the broken fence and the pieces of wood littering the ground. It was then he saw the dark shape huddled on the ground. As he drew closer, he could see it was Jamie, her hair a pool of silver under the moonlight. He ran to her and bent over her, gently lifting her head.

Brad felt her pulse and then checked her eyes. He parted her hair and gently ran his fingers over the back of her head until he found the lump, then repeated the process over her arms, legs, and ribs. He didn't feel any broken bones, but he was no expert.

He gathered her up in his arms and started to the car, his heart hammering against his chest. She shifted ever so slightly, and he tightened his hold. He refused to think about the lump on her head and focused on what had to be done.

"Hold on, sweetheart." He settled her in the seat and strapped the seat belt around her. Before closing the door, he pressed his lips against her hair.

"It's going to be all right," he murmured, praying it was true.

* * *

"I'm not leaving until I know she's all right," he said to Scott, who had joined him in the hospital waiting room an hour earlier.

Scott looked at him anxiously. "What are you going to do about the horse?"

"I don't know," Brad admitted. "I don't know." Images of Jamie clouded his vision, and he shook his head to wipe away the picture of her white face. She'd been so still.

His mind kept playing back the events of the last hour. The drive to town had passed in a blur. At the hospital, he shouldered open the double doors to the emergency room. Immediately, a nurse appeared, took in the situation, and directed him to a cubicle. He filled in umpteen forms, downed a dozen cups of coffee, and waited.

The inactivity grated at his nerves. He'd spent enough time in hospitals, waiting while his father had slowly died, to know that waiting was its own special brand of torture.

When Jim Franckum appeared, Brad sprang up. "How is she?"

"Jamie's going to be fine. She took a pretty good bump to the head and sustained some bruises, otherwise she's all right. She can go home tomorrow."

"Can I see her?"

"She's sedated now."

"I know."

The doctor hesitated. "A few minutes only."

Brad found his hands shaking as he pushed open the door. He thought he was prepared, but he'd been fooling himself. Nothing could have prepared him for the sight of Jamie lying stiller than death in the hospital bed. Nothing could have prepared him for her whiter-than-white face, only a fraction of a shade darker than the hospital-white sheet. He took a few seconds to pull himself together before crossing the room to stand beside her bed.

Smoothing the hair back from her forehead, he then traced the curve of her cheek with one finger. He smiled tenderly at the picture she made, with her soft curls framing the small face. The bandage across one temple only emphasized her fragile beauty. His mouth tightened as he remembered why she needed that bandage.

Conquistador.

That black devil had cost Brad time, trouble, not to mention a lot of money. But none of those compared with the pain and anxiety he was experiencing now.

He let his gaze rest on her face once more and tried to remember the doctor's assurance that she'd be all right. *She's strong*, he reminded himself, strong enough to stand up to him, Nate Henderson, and every other rancher around. She was the strongest woman he'd ever known.

She stirred and moaned slightly, her hands moving restlessly under the sheet. She murmured his name. A smile chased across her face. He wondered if she was thinking of him.

A few minutes later, the nurse shooed him out. He left reluctantly.

Jamie woke and looked up to find Brad slumped in the chair by her bed. Dark smudges circled his eyes, and a day's growth of beard shadowed his jaw. Weariness etched itself in every line of his face, and he had never looked more dear.

She drank in the sight of him, savoring his nearness and the opportunity to study him unobserved. She attempted to sit up. The sound roused Brad, who pulled himself up immediately.

"Hi," he greeted her. "How're you feeling?"

"A little battered." She touched her head experimentally.

"You've got a bump the size of a goose egg. Good thing you're so hard-headed."

The concern in his eyes belied his teasing words, and she summoned a smile in an attempt to reassure him. The effort cost her, and she winced.

He took her hand in his and squeezed it. "You gave us a real scare."

She grimaced. "Me too. Have you been here all night?"

"Some hatchet-faced nurse made me leave after I

knew you were going to be all right. I slipped back in this morning.''

''I didn't know visiting hours started this early.''

He grinned. ''They don't.''

She looked at her hand inside his and asked the question she'd been avoiding. ''Conquistador?''

''He's long gone. Don't worry. We'll find him.''

''Brad, please, don't let anyone hurt him. It wasn't his fault. I should have known better than to wander in there without making sure he was gone first.''

''No one's going to hurt the horse. We'll bring him back for you to tag. Then he's on his way to the high country.''

Her smile became broader. ''Thank you.''

Jamie soon regained her strength. Brad insisted she take it easy for the next few days. He spent the days at her place, taking care of the mustangs, while she dozed on the porch swing. When he brought in Conquistador, he helped her place the identifying tag in the horse's ear.

On the weekend, he took her to his place and settled her on the porch; she watched while he worked with the children. When she offered to help, he told her to rest.

''Next time,'' he promised.

She held the words close to her heart. There'd be a next time and a time after that. She had to believe it.

His patience with the children, the gentle way he placed them on the horses and eased their fears, caused tears to prick her eyes. She brushed them away as she admitted to herself what she'd already known in her heart.

She loved him.

When the last of the animals had been tagged and transported to the meadow, Brad took her there, wanting to be the first to show it to her. He tried to see it through her eyes. It wasn't much. There were a few straggly trees to provide shade. Summer-dried grass, dotted with wildflowers, carpeted the area. A jagged ridge of rocks bordered it. The mustangs grazed in the far corner.

He waited.

"It's beautiful," she said and turned to him, her eyes shinning with happiness. "Thank you for making it happen."

"Hey, it was a joint effort. You and me. We make a pretty good team, don't we?"

He waited. More depended on her answer than he wanted to admit. He cared about Jamie. He liked being with her. She was the one woman he could see spending the rest of his life with. And he was tired of being alone. He'd known a long time ago that love wasn't in the plans for him, but a life with a woman he both cared about and respected was more than appealing. He looked at her.

She nodded.

He drew her to him and cupped her cheek. "Marry me."

Chapter Nine

"Wh-what did you say?"

"Marry me."

"Yes."

"Just like that?"

She smiled. "Just like that."

He picked her up and twirled her around. "I'll make you the happiest woman alive."

"I already am." Breathless, she steadied herself against him after he lowered her to the ground. Her heart was doing somersaults, sweet tumbles of joy as she realized all she'd ever wanted was hers.

"I wasn't sure what you'd say," he said, his chin resting on her head and arms looping around her waist. "I won't ask you to give up your work. I know how important it is to you. We could even build an office on the house for you. It won't be much. At least, not at first—"

She put a finger to his lips. "Hush. None of that matters." Content, she leaned against him. "Don't you know I love you?"

She felt, more than heard, the sharp intake of breath.

She lifted her head, needing to see his face. "I love you, Brad." She waited.

He framed her face with his hands. "I care about you, Jamie. You know that."

She nodded.

"I care about you more than I ever dreamed was possible."

Still, she waited.

"I want to spend the rest of my life with you. I'll always take care of you." He spread his hands, the gesture encompassing the windswept range. "Everything I have is yours."

"I know that. But everything I want is right here." She placed her hand on his heart.

He took it and cradled it within his own. "I need you, Jamie."

She heard the hitch in his breath, the husky note in his voice that told her everything she wanted to know.

"You love me." She laced her arms around his neck and tilted her face up for a kiss. "You love me."

Gently he freed himself. "Jamie, I care about you. I need you. I want you. You have to believe me. I've never said those things to another woman."

Moved by the rough emotion in his voice, she nodded again. "I know that."

"I'm trying to be totally honest with you."

A frown puckered her brow. "I'm not sure I understand."

"I'd do anything for you. Anything but . . ."

A new fear gripped her as she started to understand. "Anything but say you love me. Is that it?" She willed him to deny the words, to laugh away her fears, to take her in his arms and tell her that he loved her as much as she loved him. But a look at his eyes confirmed what she'd already known.

He gripped her shoulders. "Isn't it enough that I asked you to marry me?"

She shook off his hands. "No, it's not enough. If you can't say the words, nothing will ever be enough. Don't you understand?"

"No, I don't." He shoved a hand through his hair. "I've offered you everything I have, everything I am, and you throw it back at me because I can't say three little words."

"You offered me everything. Everything but your love." She laughed shortly. "You know what's ironic? You already love me. I see it in your face. I feel it when you touch me. But you can't say the words. You can't force yourself to say the words because if you did, you'd be vulnerable like the rest of us. And that's the one thing you won't allow yourself to be."

She saw the denial in his eyes. Even now he was lying to himself, she reflected sadly. She mounted Mustard Seed and picked up the reins. "I love you, Brad. I always will. Nothing's going to change that. Not even you."

She shored up her determination against the hope lighting his eyes and knew she was going to destroy it with her next words. "But I can't marry you."

She looked at him and, for a moment, almost relented, her resolve threatening to crumble at the pain she saw in his face. The hope had faded from his eyes. They now wore the shuttered look she'd noticed when she first met him, the look they assumed whenever he was afraid of showing what he felt. She'd have to live with the knowledge that she'd done that.

For a moment, she wavered. Would it be so wrong to take what he was offering? He loved her. She knew it. In time, she could teach him that love could heal the pain he was carrying inside. She had love enough to wait while he accepted his own feelings. Slowly she shook her head. Unless Brad could accept that now, unless he could allow himself to be vulnerable by admitting his love, they didn't have a future. And she loved him too much to accept half a life.

Tears burned in her eyes, but she refused to wipe them away. She wasn't ashamed of them. A breaking heart deserved a few tears. Briefly she wondered whether it was possible to die from a broken heart. The way she was feeling right now, she wasn't going to bet against it.

"Good-bye, Brad." She clung to the horse's reins and resisted the urge to look back. If she did, she wasn't sure she'd have the strength to leave.

Brad stared after her as she rode off, and dug his nails into his palms. Words to call her back hovered on his lips. He'd say the words she longed to hear, and everything would be all right. Even as the thought formed, he knew he couldn't do it.

She'd asked for too much. Hadn't he offered her everything he had? Everything he'd worked for, struggled for, fought for, for the better part of his adult life. And she'd tossed it back at him, as though it were nothing.

He tried to push her image from his mind but discovered he couldn't do it. She'd looked so lovely, the sun slanting shafts of light against her hair. He'd wanted to reach out and snare a fistful of the sun-bleached curls, urging her toward him. But he'd kept his hands to himself, knowing if he touched her, he wouldn't be able to let her go.

He shaded his eyes against the harsh rays of the sun. Deliberately he turned his back on the meadow where the mustangs cavorted like playful children. It was too painful, a reminder of Jamie. Instead, he focused his gaze on the range that stretched hundreds of miles in either direction.

Heat shimmered in waves. Scorched by the late summer heat, scarred by the wind that carved jagged ridges and deep valleys into it, the land was as harsh as it was beautiful. It was also his. It was an exacting taskmaster. It demanded backbreaking work, sweat, blood, and every ounce of energy he had to give. And then some.

It had taken twelve years of his life to build the ranch into something he could be proud of. It had demanded that he sacrifice everything he had just to hold on to it.

But it hadn't demanded more than he could give.

Jamie was wrong. She'd asked for the one thing he couldn't give—love.

Brad looked at the account book and bills littering his desk and wondered when he'd become a paper pusher instead of a rancher. Each year, the ranch required more and more paperwork. If he could swing it financially, he'd hire an accountant and let *him* handle the mountain of papers.

Right now, he was putting every cent he could back into the ranch, but maybe next year . . . He turned back to the pile of bills, but again his attention wandered.

The sight of Jamie's stricken face the last time he'd seen her had imprinted itself into his mind. He remembered the trembling of her lips, the tight way she'd held her hands, the pain in her eyes, and knew it was because of him.

He felt like a jerk.

With a muttered exclamation, he shoved the papers to the floor and glared at them, as if they were somehow to blame for his foul mood.

Without Jamie, the future stretched bleakly before him. She'd made him feel whole again. She had unsnarled the tangle of hurt and abandonment inside of him, an ache he hadn't even been aware of. And she had done it unconsciously, just by loving him.

It was a healing kind of love, and he'd thrown it back in her face. He wasn't the man for her. Heck, he didn't have time for a woman in his life, least of all a woman like Jamie, who deserved everything good in life. It had taken him twelve years to turn the ranch around and make it a paying proposition, twelve years to undo the years of his father's neglect.

He sloshed some coffee into a cup and gulped it down. The liquid burned his throat, but he welcomed the pain. He focused on it, trying to forget the gnawing emptiness.

This is what he wanted. Well, wasn't it? he asked himself savagely. He'd sworn he'd never let a woman get inside his life and twist him up the way his mother had done with his father.

Words from the past echoed across the years. "I want acknowledgment of my work, some recognition from the scientific world. Do you think I like being buried in this forsaken land? There's not a laboratory in three hundred miles." After all these years, he could still hear his mother's voice, laced with bitter accusation.

He stopped. His mother. He said the words aloud and waited for the pain.

Nothing.

He tried it again. Still, nothing. The bitterness he'd carried with him for twenty-five years was gone along with the pain. Instead he felt only a quiet acceptance. His mother wasn't an evil person. She just hadn't been cut out to be a mother. Why hadn't he understood that before?

Oh, he'd known it intellectually, all right. But his heart had never been able to accept it. For twenty-five years, he'd wrestled with the pain. Why was he able to let go of it now? He searched for an answer even while knowing what it was—Jamie.

It all came back to Jamie. And Jamie was leaving the following day, leaving because of him.

He scrubbed a hand along his jaw, wondering how he was going to make it through the rest of the day. He didn't dare think about tomorrow—or all the tomorrows after that.

Unable to sit still any longer, he stood and paced, his pent-up energy finding no release. The only release, he acknowledged, would be found in Jamie's arms, the taste of her lips, and the fragrance of her hair.

Confronted with a problem, he did what he always did. He headed out to the barn and saddled Shakespeare. He gave the horse his head. As if sensing his master's mood, Shakespeare galloped over the ground, taking the fences with an easy stride that gave Brad the illusion of flying. At last they pulled to a stop at the shelter of rocks where he and Jamie had picnicked.

There, away from everyone, he dismounted and gazed over the prairie. Scrub brush, dried to the color of sage, dotted the sun-baked ground. A lizard slithered across his boot. The sky was a paintbox of color.

Brad hunkered down and dug into the ground, picking up a handful of dirt. He lifted it to his nose and inhaled deeply before letting it sift through his fingers.

The land didn't change. Generations had lived, fought, and died here. The continuity of life was found here. But the thought failed to comfort him as it had in the past. In fact, nothing brought him any relief. Work, even his hours with the kids on the weekends, didn't give the satisfaction he'd once found in it. The land, land he'd sweated blood for, no longer had the power it once had.

Without Jamie, nothing was right.

He stayed there until dusk had darkened into night. A breeze shivered over him. Shakespeare whinnied softly.

With one last look at the prairie, Brad turned. "Okay, boy. Let's go home."

Automatically she folded the clothes and packed her belongings. Her job was done. She wouldn't be coming back. Her lips quirked humorously as she remembered the vow she'd made to herself that she was here to stay. But that was before she'd met Brad. Before she'd fallen in love with him. Before he'd made it clear that he didn't want that love. She'd already made arrangements to lease the land. Later, when she could think straight, she'd decide what to do with the house.

Impatiently, she shoved the rest of the clothes into her suitcase. The sooner she left, the better. But there was something she had to do first. She needed to see the mustangs one more time. A smile flitted across her lips as she thought of their new home in the meadow.

Brad's meadow.

He'd taken her there after the last of the mustangs had been transported. It was a beautiful place, a place to dream dreams . . . a place to find love.

And she had found it.

The memory caused her throat to tighten. Brad was everything she'd ever wanted. She thrust away the memories before the tears could start again. She'd wasted enough time crying. She'd have a lifetime of regrets. She didn't need to dwell on them now.

Before she could talk herself out of it, she stripped off her traveling clothes and pulled on a pair of jeans and shirt.

In the heat of late August, the land was hard and unyielding. Desert-yellow, it could be cruel, exacting a price from those not experienced in its ways.

But it was also magnificent. Its stark beauty pulled at her just as it had that first time so many summers ago. Her need to see the mustangs had her urging her horse faster. She felt the change in the air. It seemed fresher. Mustard Seed must have sensed the difference too for she whickered. Jamie patted her neck.

It grew cooler as they climbed until at last they were picking their way over the rocky ridge that rimmed the meadow. Here, the land, fed by a small spring, blossomed with color. A shrill trumpeting had her standing in the stirrups, straining to see in the distance.

Conquistador led the mustangs, his arrogance not a whit changed by his recent captivity. He stopped, ears pricked, head cocked. Apparently satisfied that nothing threatened him or his herd, he whinnied for the others to join him.

Jamie watched him, moved, as always, by his proud bearing. He was as beautiful as the land.

He belonged here. Just as she did. *She belonged here*. She'd paid the price . . . as her grandfather had . . . as Brad had.

"I belong here." She laughed.

"Do you hear that, Conquistador? I belong here. You tried to scare me off. Brad tried to run me off. He almost succeeded."

This was her home.

And if Brad couldn't see that, then it was up to her to convince him of it.

She'd never been a quitter before. She didn't intend to start now.

Brad was just going to have to accept it. She was here to stay. She loved him, and he loved her. It was up to her to make him see it.

The heaviness that had settled around her heart for the last week lifted. She'd spent too many days moping around feeling sorry for herself. She intended to change that—starting now.

His head heavy and aching, Brad forced himself out of bed.

Sleep had eluded him for the past week. If he was lucky, he managed to snatch a few hours near morning when his exhausted mind finally gave up the struggle and succumbed to the oblivion of sleep.

Inevitably, he awoke to the depressing memory that nothing had changed. Jamie was leaving. And he was letting her go.

He had no choice, he reminded himself. The only other alternative was to admit that he loved her. And that he could not do.

Could not or would not?

He pushed the thought away. He headed for the shower and tried to remember what it had felt like to be happy. He had an uneasy feeling that memories of the feeling might be all he had to look forward to in the future.

Although he'd told her dozens of times in the past not to bother fixing breakfast for him, Mrs. Milligan had ham and eggs waiting. He forced a smile to his lips while groaning inwardly. The last thing he felt like doing was eating. Dutifully, though, he pushed the food around on his plate, aware that he wasn't fooling her.

"It was real good," he told her as he started out the door.

Rather than the scolding he expected, she gave him a sympathetic look, which had the effect of making him feel worse than ever. He headed outside. A breeze stirred the air, and he inhaled deeply.

Work waited for him, but he found no pleasure in the thought. He headed toward the barn, where Shakespeare greeted him with a loud snort. Brad scratched the big gelding behind the ears. "Come on, boy, we've got some fences that need mending."

Automatically he gathered up the tools he'd need and saddled Shakespeare.

The ride had done him good.

He lifted his gaze to study the horizon. Pink and orange streaked the sky, a vivid contrast to the brown of the scorched earth. Sunrise was his favorite time of day. Then, with the air still retaining a hint of the night's chill and the heat of the sun only a promise, he could believe in dreams.

Jamie believed in dreams; she even had him *wanting* to believe. He allowed himself a small smile. Since when had he started believing in dreams?

Dreams.

Jamie.

The two went together.

What had she said about his dream of turning his ranch into a full-time place for children with disabilities? A frown puckered his brow as he tried to remember.

If you want something hard enough, you'll make it happen.

Well, he wanted it.

You have to say it aloud.

Feeling foolish, he said the words. "I want to turn the ranch into a full-time place for children with disabilities." He repeated the words.

Something stirred inside of him—a quickening of excitement that made him believe he could make his dream come true. If he did, he'd have Jamie to thank.

Jamie believed in dreams, just as she believed in love. *Love*—the word he'd shied away from for so many years, the word that Jamie had needed him to say, the word he couldn't say.

So what was he left with?

Nothing. He tried reminding himself that that's what he'd had before she found her way into his life, but the emptiness he experienced now was that much more painful because he knew what fulfillment felt like.

He shook his head in derision. Here he was thinking about dreams. Well, dreams weren't going to mend the fence or anything else. He shrugged off his shirt and started to work.

An hour later, he paused to wipe the sweat from his neck. The sound of hoofbeats had him looking up. He grunted a greeting as Scott hobbled his horse.

"Good morning to you too," Scott said. "I can see you're in the same sunny mood that you've favored us with all week."

Brad scowled. "Don't you have some work to do?"

"Nope. I've got nothing but time," Scott said, leaning against the railing as Brad reinforced a fence pole. "Why'd you let Jamie go?"

Brad's expression hardened. "I didn't let her do anything. She left because she wanted to."

"You're a fool."

His hands tightened around the pole. "You're pushing it, little brother."

"Maybe it's time someone did. You've been king of the range for so long you've forgotten how to be anything else."

Brad spun around. "If you're looking for a fight, you don't have to look any further."

Scott straightened and planted his hands on his hips. "Take your best shot."

Brad's anger drained out of him. He couldn't fight his brother, especially when he knew that Scott was right. He turned back to his work.

Scott picked up the wire and held it taut as Brad twisted it around the pole. They worked together, speaking only when necessary until Scott broke the silence. "Jamie did something you didn't like."

Brad paused, and the wire fell slack. "What're you talking about?"

"Love, big brother. She fell in love with you. Then she had the guts to tell you about it." Scott shook his head. "I've never seen you afraid of anything. But that scared you. It scared you so bad you couldn't even tell her that you love her."

"I don't—"

"You lied to Jamie. You can lie to me. But don't lie to yourself. It won't work."

"I'm not lying . . ." Brad stopped. He looked at his hands. They were shaking. He curled them at his sides in an attempt to control their trembling. "You're wrong," he said at last, finally stuffing his hands inside his pockets.

A glance at Scott's face told Brad he hadn't fooled his brother one bit.

"You love her," Scott repeated.

Brad wanted to deny it, meant to, but the protest died on his lips. "I love her."

The words came with such ease that he wondered

how he hadn't realized it before. He loved her. He loved Jamie. Of course. That's why he'd fought so long and hard against his attraction to her. That's why he'd failed to understand what he was feeling. Love had been so lacking in his life that he didn't recognize it even when it was staring him in the face.

Everything was simple now. He'd tell her that he loved her and . . . He shook his head, remembering that she was due to leave today. He looked up to find the sun high in the sky. "She's gone."

"Yeah," Scott agreed. "What're you going to do about it?"

For the first time in a week, Brad smiled. It felt good. "Go after her."

"Go for it."

Brad clapped his brother on the shoulder. "How'd you get so smart, little brother?"

Scott grinned. "I had a good teacher. He also just happens to be my big brother."

Brad handed the hammer to Scott and unhitched Shakespeare from the fence. "Wish me luck."

"I don't think you're going to need it," Scott said.

"By the way," Brad called over his shoulder. "You get to fix the fence."

"You just be sure you bring home my soon-to-be sister-in-law."

Brad headed to Jamie's house on the chance he'd catch her before she left. He gave a quick sigh of relief when he saw her car parked in front of the house. A quick check of the barn revealed that Mustard Seed was gone.

Where had she gone?

"Come on, boy," he urged Shakespeare. "We've got a lady to find."

Without the walls he'd erected around himself, he felt freer than he had in years. Happiness awaited him. All he had to do was to convince Jamie to recognize that he loved her. No, first he had to find her. He didn't let himself think about what would happen after that.

He found her there on the crest of the ridge overlooking the meadow where the mustangs now resided. He remembered the first time he'd taken her there. She'd been beautiful that morning, her face flushed from excitement, her hair a shining beacon under the sun.

Brad paused, watching her now. Her head bent, she was a lonely figure, silhouetted against the darkening sky. He lifted his gaze to study the gathering clouds. It was going to storm.

He remembered another time, another storm. He and Jamie had fought their way out of it. Maybe together they could find their way out of the mess he'd created with his stubbornness.

And his fear.

He slapped Shakespeare gently on the flank. "Come on. Let's go get her."

Brad curbed his impatience as the big gelding picked his way carefully over the rocks. Shakespeare neighed in protest as Brad pulled tighter on the reins. "Sorry, boy."

Within a few minutes they were only yards away from Jamie. She couldn't have missed the sound of their approach. Still, she didn't turn around.

Suddenly unsure of himself, he dismounted and hobbled Shakespeare.

He searched for something to say and settled for a simple hello. *Good going, Kincaid. Can't you think of anything more original than that?*

"Hi."

Her eyes were wary, he noted. He didn't blame her.

"How'd you find me?" she asked.

"I took a chance you might be here."

"Why?"

"Why what?" He knew he was stalling, but he couldn't help it. He was scared. What if she told him to take a flying leap?

"Why'd you come?"

"Because I don't want you to go."

"Why?"

The time had come. "I love you."

"Don't," she said.

"Didn't you hear me?" he asked, taking her hands in his. "I love you." He still marveled at the words. He'd shunned them, afraid of what they'd mean if he dared utter them aloud. Now, they fell off his tongue with an ease that amazed him.

"Don't say it if you don't mean it," Jamie begged. "I couldn't bear it."

"I've never said anything I don't mean. I don't intend to start now."

She looked at him, her gaze searching his face.

He resisted the temptation to take her in his arms. If she came to him, it had to be because *she* wanted it.

What she saw in his face must have given her the answer she sought, for at last she smiled. "You love me."

"That's what I've been trying to tell you."

"What made you change your mind?"

"It wasn't a question of changing my mind. It was . . . " He paused, wanting her to understand what he'd only begun to. "I was afraid."

"Of me?"

"Of loving you." He drew a deep breath. "Of loving anyone. I kept remembering my parents. They loved each other . . . once. But it died and left something ugly and bitter in its place. For a long time, too long, I couldn't see beyond that. My mother—"

"Didn't know what she was giving up. It wasn't your fault. It wasn't your fault," she repeated, her voice soft.

"I know that. Now." He cupped her face in his palms. "You helped me see that."

She shook her head. "I didn't do anything."

He put a finger to her lips. "But you did. You loved me. Even when I tried to push you away, you kept right on loving me."

She laughed softly. "I didn't have any choice in the matter."

"Neither do I." He kissed her then.

She lifted a hand to cup his cheek. "We're not your parents."

He caught her hand and brought it to his lips, drawing her to him at the same time. "No. We're not."

"We're us—you and me."

"Can you forgive me for being a pigheaded fool?"

In answer, she kissed him. "What made you look for me here?" she asked after long minutes.

He smiled. "I knew how much you loved the mustangs. I took a chance you'd want to see them again."

"I'm glad you came," she said softly. "I almost left." Her voice turned husky.

"What made you change your mind?" he asked.

"I remembered the first time I ever came here. It was with a man. A very special man. A man who cared about what happened to the mustangs even when he pretended to deny it, even when they were costing him his dream. A man who cares about kids with problems. A man who—"

"A man who almost let you go," he cut in. "He was a fool."

She shook her head. "Never that."

"He was a fool to let you go."

"But he came to his senses."

"Yeah," Brad said, closing his lips over hers once more. "He came to his senses."

"I'm glad." She threw him a teasing look. "I'd made up my mind to stay. I was going to convince you that you loved me even if it took the rest of my life. I'm glad it's not going to take that long."

"Not half as glad as I am."

The light died from her eyes.

He suddenly grew afraid. What wasn't she telling him? "What is it?"

"Nothing."

He cupped her chin. "I can see it in your eyes. Something's troubling you. Tell me . . . please."

"I've been thinking about your plans to turn the ranch into a full-time place for children with disabilities."

"It's hardly a plan. Only a dream. Maybe . . . someday."

"I told you once that I believe in dreams."

"I remember."

"Have you ever thought of taking on a partner?"

"It'd be great. The problem is no one would be willing to work for what I can afford to pay."

"I wouldn't be so sure about that. It ought to be someone who shares your dream. Someone to work toward it with you. Someone who can help with the kids and the horses."

He was beginning to understand. "Did you have anyone in mind?"

"As a matter of fact, I do. Me."

"You'd do that?"

"Of course I would."

"But your job . . . I can't ask you to give it up. You spent all your life preparing for it."

"You're not asking. I'm volunteering. I want to help make your dream come true. If you'll let me."

He looked at her, afraid to believe what he was hearing. She'd given him so much already. How could he ask for any more? But the love he saw shining in her eyes confirmed that he'd heard correctly.

"Our dream," he corrected softly. "Yours and mine."

She must have understood what he was saying for she raised her hand to touch his cheek. "We'll make it come true, Brad. We can do it. Anything's possible . . . as long as we're together."

With Jamie at his side, he could do anything. Energy surged through him. He covered her hand with his own, drawing her closer to him. "Together."